the flower in the skull

the flower in the skull
in the
skull

KATHLEEN ALCALÁ

*For Pat —
always,
K. Alcalá
19 June, 1998*

CHRONICLE BOOKS
SAN FRANCISCO

JACKET: Painting copyright © 1998 by Claire B. Cotts. "Margaret and Lupé Selene," acrylic on canvas, private collection. Background by Andrew Faulkner Illustration.

A portion of this novel was published in an early form under the title "Walking Home" in *The Americas Review*, Volume 23, Number 3–4, Fall-Winter 1995.

Library of Congress Cataloging-in-Publication Data:

Alcalá, Kathleen, 1954–
　　Flower in the skull : a novel / by Kathleen Alcalá.
　　192 p.　 14 x 20.3 cm.
　　ISBN 0-8118-1916-7
　　1. Mexican American women—California—Los Angeles—Fiction.
2. Indian women—North America—Fiction.　3. Opata Indians—Fiction.
I. Title.
　　PS3551.L287F56　1998
　　813'.54—dc21　　　　　　　　　　　　 97-32553
　　　　　　　　　　　　　　　　　　　　　 CIP

Printed in the United States of America
Designed by Laura Lovett
Typeset by Neal Elkin, On Line Typography

Distributed in Canada by Raincoast Books
8680 Cambie Street
Vancouver, British Columbia V6P 6M9

10 9 8 7 6 5 4 3 2 1

Chronicle Books
85 Second Street
San Francisco, California 94105

Web Site: www.chroniclebooks.com

This novel is dedicated to the people of the Sonoran Desert.

acknowledgments

I would like to thank Anne Woosley and Allan McIntyre of the Amerind Foundation, and the Department of American Indian Studies at the University of Arizona for making their time and resources available to me. I would also like to acknowledge Artist Trust and the Washington State Arts Commission for financial support, and Hedgbrook Farm for time and a place to write.

Many people have worked to preserve and pass on the cultures of the Sonoran Desert, among them Thomas Hinton, Patricia Preciado Martin, Edward and Rosalyn Spicer, Thomas Sheridan, Gary Paul Nabhan, James S. Griffith, and Bernardo Fontana. The work of Ofelia Zepeda and Leslie Marmon Silko have also been an inspiration to me. I hope the interested reader will seek out their work as well.

I would like to thank my agent, Kim Witherspoon, for her efforts to get my work published, and my editor, Jay Schaefer, for his continued faith and patience.

the flower in the skull

Y en medio de esos cambios interiores
tu cráneo lleno de una nueva vida,
en vez de pensamientos dará flores.

Manuel Acuña, de "Ante un cadaver"

Amid those internal changes
Your skull fills with a new life,
and instead of thoughts, has flowers.

Manuel Acuña, from "Before a Corpse"

·I·

concha

Something Precious

In the desert, deep inside the spiny center of the cactus, nests a bird no bigger than my finger. While the sharp thorns fend off animals that would eat the eggs, the parent birds come and go at will. And this was my mother's name, "living at the heart of the spiny cactus," Chiri, what others would call Hummingbird. The last time I saw her was on the way to Casas Grandes.

In Sonora is a river called Moctezuma, and a village there was our home, just before the Moctezuma meets the Yaqui River. My mother and her sister owned rancherías, and their husbands and sons raised corn and wheat and cotton and many good things to eat. The soil was good and the water from the river was sweet, the sweetest I ever tasted.

My name at that time was Shark's Tooth from the Sea, which means "something precious." The Opata used to trade good baskets to the Seri for shark's teeth to decorate their clothes and baskets, and when I was born, my mother's family named me after this rare and beautiful object. It meant that I was strong and fierce and wild and beautiful, all things that the

Opata wanted in their baby girls. My name also held the promise of water, which made it even more precious.

The women wove baskets and ground corn and carried babies and sang songs. And the chiefs of peace would gather the people in the center place each evening and tell the stories of the place where we lived, of sacred mountains and rivers, of the miracles of Saint Francis, and the lives of good men. The story of the life of a good man, they used to say, is worth as much as a good rainstorm.

This is what we left. We left all of this behind when the fighting got too bad, when the crops were burned, when the villages were burned and the cattle stolen, when the young girls were kidnapped and the men were captured or shot. All of this we left behind when the fighting between the Mexican Army and the Yaqui got too bad, and the Mexicans couldn't tell the Opata from the Yaqui, and treated us just as bad as they treated the Yaqui, who had a vision of their own country, an Indian country separate from the rest of Mexico, where the Yaqui and the Opata and the Mayo and Pima and all the others could own their own land and live in peace.

This is what my people left when they picked up their feet and put on their bundles and their babies and walked north to Tucson and Nogales and the northern Opatería.

I did not know if I could do this. I did not know if I could pick up my feet, put on my sandals, and walk the long, long way, the singing way, north to the river people of the Santa Cruz. My mother and brother and sisters stood, bundles on their backs and their heads, and looked at me. If I stayed, here where the desert sang for me, where the trees grew and the birds lived and every rock and lizard was a companion to me, if I stayed, they told me, I would die. They will come for us again, and this time, they said, they might do more to me than before. The Spanish/Mexicans would kill me for being a Yaqui, or the Apache would kill me for not being one of them.

We had no choice. We had to pick up our feet and put on our sandals and walk. Away from our homes, our fields, away from our mountains and valleys, away from our rivers and sacred places, away, even, from our sky. We walked to where the Pima and Papago lived, where the Apache had fought and lost. We walked to where the Americans lived, and hoped to live in peace. We were not fighters, we were not horse people, although we loved our horses. We were river people, and just needed a little land and water for our milpas.

There was room here now, and Mexican and American ranchers who needed help, because the Apache had been killed or sent far away. Much of this land had once belonged to the Opata, had been where they grew corn and cotton and squash and beans, but because of the Apache and their appetite for blood, white and Indian alike, the Northern Opata had abandoned their rancherías and fled south to join their brothers in the mountains.

Now the Opata returned—no longer owners of their own rancherías, since they had no papers to prove such things, but as hired hands on the same land. All we had were our strong backs. And this was because the Mexican Army had become worse than the Apache, or at least not much better.

This is the story of my journey to Tucson, where I would find both happiness and sorrow. This is the story of my people, the Opata, who once numbered as many as the saguaro of the desert, and who once farmed many rancherías and had many villages, but are now just a few, and scattered far and wide from their home and the constellations that knew them.

Hu'uki

In the dry season I sat in the hu'uki and watched my mother
weave.

First Chiri soaked the palm leaves, then split them into
long, narrow strips. These she soaked as well, submerging them
in a large, shallow bowl of water at one side of the hu'uki.

I remember the summer that the women built it. They dug
a circular pit in the ground, about four feet deep. It took a long
time. They moved the earth one basketful at a time, emptying
each close to the river, where the men spread it flat with a hoe.

When the pit was deep enough, the women climbed in and
pounded it flat, pressing the earth with the soles of their feet,
laughing and holding up their skirts, until it was smooth and
even. They danced in a spiral motion, from the center to the
outside, so that the floor of the hu'uki would be even and balanced, tuned like a drum to the center of the earth.

Then they went to the trees and cut supple willow branches,
planting one end in the ground and bending it over to the top
of the pit, planting and bending another over until there were

enough to tie together and form a round roof. Then they wove branches in between, singing and laughing the whole time, in the old way. They were singing, but I felt that singing in the old way was the same as what the maestros called praying.

We sang over the hu'uki, and made it a good place to weave, a sacred place where the women went and worked in the summer, weaving the palm mats and baskets and hats while the men went to work in the fields.

This is the way it had been all my life, and I felt the singing wash over me as a child, as warm and comforting as my mother's hand on my head.

Every time I went into the hu'uki, I remembered that singing, as though the words hung in the air, the breath woven into the roof like the branches, caught in the blue throats of the tiny lizards that sought refuge there.

The air was different inside the hu'uki, dark and rich, full of women and earth smells. I always felt larger when I entered its embrace, as though floating in an atmosphere of earth, water, and song. While I was just a small girl outside, someone who carried water a long way while the boys watched, I became large and dark and humid inside, like the hu'uki itself, as though I became a part of it.

The hu'uki belonged to the women of my mother's family. Chiri always sat in the same place, in the same way, a clean petate beneath her. She sat to the right of the door, facing the center, the bowl of palm strips to her right. If she was alone in the hu'uki, she was silent. But if I or my sisters or other women came in, she would sometimes sing or tell stories.

The men never went in or near the hu'uki because it was a special place. The women worked with them in the fields most of the year, but in the dry season the women worked in the hu'ukis, and the men stayed in the fields. This is how it had always been.

Although everyone was always busy outside—planting and

harvesting, feeding the animals, cooking food, bringing water, weaving cloth, making clothes — time seemed to slow down in the hu'uki. It was used during the dry season, because that's where the women wove, and the palm strips had to stay moist and pliant in order to weave well. In the spring the women of the village took much of what they had made to the Fiesta de San Francisco in Magdalena, where they would sell or trade it for other goods. This was the one time of year when we saw people from other valleys, from places farther away than someone could travel in a day.

All year I looked forward to the dry season, fall to spring, because that is when we spent more time in the hu'uki, and Chiri would tell us stories. This is when I learned the stories of my family, the singing way, and the ways of plants and animals, and most mysterious of all, the ways of people.

I learned about my own people, and about the Pimas and the Mayo, the Yaquis to the south and the Papago at the northern edge of the Opatería, places I never expected to visit. This is also where I learned the way of the vecinos, the neighbors who were Mexican, not Indian, who came to farm and ranch and be soldiers for the army in Sonora. Sometimes they were friendly, as when they fought the Apache with us, and sometimes the vecinos attacked the Opata. All of these things I learned from my mother, and it seemed like a lot, but in later years, I wished that I had listened more carefully.

There was a village in the Sierra Occidental, high on the side of a mountain, the water running swiftly below. It was a village of proud and beautiful people, people who some say had come from the north long ago. This is one of the stories that my mother told. They were tall and straight and some of the children had red hair, like the children of the sun, like the god-kings of Cuzco, far to the south.

The village grew corn and even a little cotton down by the river, but mostly they traded for cotton like the other tribes, even though they were part of the Opata. The village was strong, and their singing lines were clean and true. God was good to them, and they had many children.

But a time came when God was not pleased. Mexican soldiers came from the capital, and the people fled but were caught or shot or driven away. No one knew what they wanted, food or land or gold. Probably gold, because wherever there were rumors of gold, there followed death like a shrieking bird with claws extended to rip the flesh from the body.

The soldiers came and killed everyone—everyone they could find, but two children escaped, a brother and sister with reddish hair. These two, about nine and ten years old, were found days later by people from another village—starving, stunned, but alive—and taken in. A mine was opened at the place where the devastated village had been.

An Indian family raised the two children as their own, telling them what had happened, because they must not forget. The children had to remember that they were the last of their people. The boy and girl grew straight and tall, like cornstalks with red silk hair.

When they were old enough, the boy and girl decided to have a baby, since they were the last of their family, since everyone was lost but the two of them. When the village saw that the girl was pregnant, and knew what they had done, as brother and sister, they were cast out of the village. They walked and walked until they found a village of people who did not know them, and there the girl gave birth to a baby girl. The brother and sister raised the baby girl in that village, keeping their secret from the people so that they would not be sent away. Another daughter was born as well. The children did not have red hair like the brother and sister, but the parents were very proud of them anyway. The children were the last of their family, the last of their kind, and in them ran the blood of ancient kings. They named one Chiri, meaning Hummingbird, messenger from the dead, and the other Francisca, known as Pancha.

The girls were wild and strong, and when Chiri was old enough, the brother and sister, who had lived out their lives as man and wife, took her and her sister to a different village to find her a husband. She was wild and strong and the boys in the village where she grew up were afraid of her. In the new village, farther north, a boy was found who was strong enough for her, who could balance her power, and he led her back to the village campfire to be his wife.

And this was the story of my parents that my mother, Chiri, told me, and the story of her parents as well. For it was my father who was strong enough to be her husband, and her parents who had been the last of their family, having lost everything to the soldiers farther south, in the village of Tónichi. And so my mother had been brought to Tepupa, near where we lived in Los Arbolitos, and where the sun rose and set every day across our valley. This is the story Chiri told me as she wove palm in the hu'uki, wove palm with words to lodge in the thatch above us, to rest in the ears of the lizards that rustled and moved all around.

And this is a story that my mother told me. When the first people lived here, the world was always dark. Everyone worked and slept in darkness. But, an old woman told my mother, the old people decided to do something about it. They were tired of always living in the dark. So they made the sun and the moon at Cobora. The people who lived there called together all the people from the surrounding villages. Then they built two fires and began to tickle each other. They tickled and tickled each other until two people were found not to be ticklish, a man and a woman, no matter how much they were tickled. The others took the man and threw him into the fire, and he became the sun; then they threw the woman into the other fire, and she burned up and became the moon.

The sun appeared first in the west and proceeded to the east, there to begin his course back across the sky. The moon followed afterwards from the same direction, always following in the footsteps of her husband, the sun.

But they did not yet have a name for the sun and the moon. In order to create names for the sun and moon, not only the people of Cobora and Batesopa, but those of all the surrounding pueblos, including Tamichopa, were summoned together. After the burning of the man and the woman, the old people sat together all night in order to invent a name for the sun. They thought and they thought, and many names were called out, but none was the right name for the sun.

At sunrise, they had not yet found a name for the great, shining being that raised his head above the horizon and began to cast his light everywhere. When that light reached where they sat, a cricket sitting under a metate near an old woman suddenly began to chirp: Ta-senide, Ta-senide. The old woman crouching nearby called "Listen!" And they all stopped and listened, and agreed that that was the right name for the sun. Thereafter they called the sun "Ta" and they looked for the cricket and placed it in a safe spot, and fed it and cared for it until it died of old age.

This is how I learned the name of Ta the sun, and Metza, his wife, the moon. And this is where my mother told me of their children, the morning star and the evening star. These were the stories that my mother told me when I was little, when I was just learning to soak and split the palm leaves evenly and smoothly, so that we could weave them into petates and hats and baskets to use ourselves, or trade to our vecinos, or sell at the Fiesta de San Francisco.

My mother, too, was one person inside the hu'uki and another outside. Inside, she would speak to me and sing, and even listen to my questions. She seemed quieter than she was outside, for my mother had a loud, high voice that carried a long way. When she laughed, everyone knew who it was. My Tía Pancha would cover her mouth and laugh inside.

Before we were born, my mother was like her name, Hummingbird, traveling around Sonora to sell her baskets, returning each season to El Arbolito to weave and sing until it was too dark to see. My father would go with her to sell the baskets, and he would just stand back and watch as my mother talked and laughed. It was only after her children were born that Chiri spent most of her time in the village, and no longer walked among strangers at every chance. Until this time the other women of the village had looked at her with dissapproving eyes, for Opata women are supposed to stay in their villages and take care of the houses and animals and make sure that their husbands farm the land. They are not supposed to walk in the houses of other people, and even though her husband traveled with her, Chiri was seen as bold and maybe scandalous.

Before, most of the Opata grew cotton to trade or sell. Until a few years before, my father said, the Indians had come from all over Sonora and from the northern pueblos to trade for chinapa, as cotton was called, with the Opata. An Opata woman could set up a loom around four sticks in the ground and weave any pattern she could look at. A sickness had come to the cotton some years before, so only a few people still tried to grow it.

After that, the Mexican government had started trying to tax the Indians who came to trade, so they had stopped their annual trip from the north. More people, like my mother and Tía Pancha, harvested and wove palm for their baskets and petates. Chiri did not even like cotton. It cut her hands, she complained, but her hands were tough and deft as she dampened the palm strips and wove her baskets as tight as cloth. She wore her hair long and wild, her dresses pinned on without regard for her looks, but her baskets held a concentration and symmetry that glowed with power. In her baskets you could see her strength.

My mother sold her baskets at fiestas for a high price, or gambled them away at the games. Her appearance at a game of bones with one or two of her baskets drew cries of joy, and the bone-throwers welcomed the sight of her. She sang in a high, nasal voice, tossing her head back with her eyes shut, and even we, her children, made fun of her to each other. But I would miss that voice many nights when I was no longer young, remembering the tangle of warm limbs in the small jacal, a smoky green fire burning outside to drive mosquitos away. I remember drifting in and out of sleep to my mother's voice, the deep, even breathing of my brothers and sisters around me.

I was the firstborn in my family. After my two sisters were born, Chiri had less time for me. I already had a brother, but he was quiet and shy and clung to our mother's skirt wherever she went. He was a shadow to her, and only went with me if he had to. Chiri loved all of us, but my brother and I were just a part of her, there but not there. Her next two children she saw in a different way.

Choqui and Segua were born after a long night of labor, during which the village women burned candles and prayed. When it turned out that Chiri had twin girls, and that they both were strong enough to live, everyone was very happy. They were beautiful, tiny babies, with black hair that stood straight up from their heads when they were born, and never fell out as they got older. Their names meant Star and Flower, two holy names that would give them strength.

During that night, while waiting outside with other men of the village, my father made a manda that he would be a pascola dancer every Easter after that if my mother would live. He was true to his word, and every year after that he took time out from our fields to dance the pascola dances for a long time leading up to Easter, and also when there was the funeral of a child, for pascolas danced at the funeral of a child or an unmarried man or woman. This is the way it had always been, even before the priests like Father Kino came and gave many new names to the old things, or tried to get rid of them altogether.

Choqui and Segua took up all of our mother's time, and she did not have enough milk to nurse my brother Rufino. I would hold him and offer him goat's milk, but he would cry and cry and wanted to push the baby girls away from our mother. I made him toys and tried to sing him the songs that our mother sang, but he would have none of it. He became a quiet boy who did not trust people.

Chiri made tiny dresses for my sisters and braided their hair in tiny braids. My father was very proud of his family. There were now more mouths to feed, however, and we had to work hard in the milpas. My father looked forward to having Rufino become old enough to help him more.

A few years after, my youngest brother, Beto, was born. He was the one I cared for the most, because my mother spent so much time on the other girls. Although I was young, Beto was almost like my own son. He was a happy child, and although he often kept all of us awake at night, we forgave him during the day for his laughter and his sweet ways.

Beto was the one who answered questions, and the longer time went on, the more questions all of us had.

The Boy with the Calendar in His Head

Beto was four when his great gift became apparent.

Although he was often sick, my mother protected him as her youngest, even when others said that he should be left alone in the hills for nature to take her course.

Since he had been a year old, Beto had suffered from fits and fevers, and Chiri had tied a red string around his wrist to protect him from the spirits.

But the spirits must have visited Beto nonetheless, because when he was old enough to relate such things, he told us of a dream he had during one of his fevers.

Beto dreamed, he said, of a place north and west where the trail rose up steeply from the desert. There, in an isolated group of hills, was an oasis where our own people used to go. It had much water, and beautiful fruit trees grew all around. The trees swarmed with tiny green parrots that rose in clouds when approached by people. The chachalacas filled the air with their chattering.

He did not know the name of the place, said Beto, but knew

that it had been thirty-four years since any of our people had been there.

We listened to this dream in astonishment, then took him to the oldest man in the village, a cripple who had lived through many battles with the Apache.

"Es cierto," he said. "We used to go there in better times. But it is a long way, with no good water before you get to the good springs of the place.

"But how could you tell, niño," said the old man to Beto, "how many years it has been since anyone has been there?"

Beto lifted his hand and pointed in the air. "I could tell by the sun in my dream," he said. "By the place of the sun in the sky."

And we marveled at this, because in the old days, it was said, people could tell many things from the sun and his wife, the moon, and even from their children, the stars.

And so my brother Beto came to be known as the boy with the calendar in his head. People began to come to him with questions about the past, how many years since so and so died, or who used to farm the milpas near the abandoned village of such and such a place. Sometimes Beto had an answer, and sometimes not. Just as often, his answer concerned the future as much as the past.

And this was a great marvel to all of us. We seldom received news of even the past or the present. El Arbolito relied on outsiders who passed through to bring letters or news from other villages. And here was someone right in the village who could tell what would happen in the future.

People came with practical questions like "Will my daughter have children soon?" "Will the crops be good this year?" but Beto's answers were not always straightforward. We came to see his answers as riddles, as puzzles to be worked on and thought about as we went through our days. After one of Beto's pronouncements, we would think and think about what he had to say, and at the end of the day, one person might greet another by saying, "Perhaps the chickens stand for days of the week," or "The ripe melon could mean a pregnancy."

Each time someone came with a question, he or she brought a little something to eat, or a petate, or a sweet. Not too much, since he was only a child, but enough that we had a little more than before, and no one said that Beto should be left alone in the hills anymore.

At night, Beto slept by our mother's side so that she could wake up if he began to shake, and fend off the spirits that were attracted to the ancient gifts that had taken up residence in my brother. His cries and shakes were hard on all of us at night, and more and more my father took his petate outside to sleep under the stars.

One day a woman came with a weaving she had made herself. It was small but very fine. She gave it to my mother and waited patiently as she was given a little something to eat, but we could tell that she was not hungry and probably had a question for my brother. Sometimes these questions were of a personal nature, so I took my two sisters and we went a little way from the house to play.

Finally my mother said "Díme, is there something you would like to ask my son?"

"Por favor," she stammered, looking at her hands in her lap, "can you tell me who the father of Rafaela's next child will be?"

This was a question that surprised even my mother, and I don't know if my brother had an answer. But the question was one to stump even a powerful curandero, much less a little boy.

There was a woman in our village who was muy blanca. She said that her father had been French, from when the French tried to take over Mexico and had landed on the west coast, and that she had been born in Guaymas. I don't know if she spoke any French, but she spoke Spanish. She lived across the river from the rest of the village in a house with stone walls. Most of us had walls made out of petates, although my father had built one stone wall and a raised hearth on the outside of it for cooking. Our roof beams rested on this wall, and the rest of the house was built from there. It was very nice. On cold nights, the stones stayed warm from the fire, and we could sleep against that wall.

Rafaela's house had been there before, but all fallen down. When she came to live in our village, she got the men to restore the house for her and put a new roof on it. Rafaela was like that — she could get men to do things for her. And that is how she came to have so many children.

Rafaela was also different from us in many other ways. She wore bright colors. In a village where the young girls wore white and the women wore black skirts and white blouses, Rafaela stood out like a wild bird in a flock of chickens. She wore green blouses and red skirts, blue skirts and purple blouses, striped rebozos and yellow dresses.

In some ways, this was a good idea, because Rafaela had her children without being married. It was not uncommon to marry and then take a different husband, but everyone agreed you should get married at least once before having children.

"Don't talk too much to the boys," the women would say to their daughters, "or you will end up like that French woman across the river." When I was little, this made me think that talking too much was what made you have children.

Rafaela had never married that anyone knew of, but she had children just the same. Some of them were light like her, and some dark. People had a good idea who the fathers were, for there was more than one. Some of the fathers were married to other women, and some were not. At least one man whom people thought was a man who loved other men claimed to have a child by Rafaela, and in fact, one little chaparito did look like him.

Rafaela dressed her children like parrots, too, which was difficult in a town where dyed goods were hard to come by. She would sweet-talk a man called El Gusano and roll cigarettes for him, and he would give her leftover ribbons and pieces of cloth he was unable to sell to others.

El Gusano used to come on horseback to our village to trade. He always came with a lot of money and brought mescal for the men, and even the women who wanted it. He would take someone aside and talk in a low voice so no one could hear, his big black Stetson with the rattlesnake band pulled low over his eyes, so all you could see was smoke. Pretty soon that man was nodding, and you could see that they were counting things up. Sometimes El Gusano brought canned food or tobacco, things that were hard to get in our valley unless a relative sent them. Men asked him for more hats like his own and he always promised to bring them, but he never did.

The children called him El Gusano because he looked at you in a way that made you feel like worms were crawling over your body. Even though he brought new things, we did not like that man. Once he came and took a girl away, crying. The adults said she was going away to be married, but nobody looked happy when they said it. A girl would have a wedding in her village if this were true, but the girl who went with El Gusano never returned to have a wedding.

The women said nothing against Rafaela, at least nothing that the men could hear, and she stayed to her property on the other side of the river. When it flooded, they were sometimes trapped there for a few days, in a little place where the skirt of the river widened for a few yards. The people in the valley could see Rafaela and her children over there, perched like a flock of birds on a few rocks or on the roof of the house, their belongings surely soaked. But each time it happened, Rafaela scraped the mud out of her stone house and spread her things to dry, and her few rows of corn and squash would grow better than ever.

Rufino, my other brother, began to resent the attention that was paid to our youngest brother. Rufino was handsome, almost a man now, and had always received a lot of favors from the women of the village. He was lazy, though, and did not like to help our father in the milpas. So when Beto began his dreaming, Rufino, I think, felt forgotten. This was when he began to spend more time with our cousins and drink mescal and tesguino when he could get it.

This is why Rufino was not with our father when he was taken away with the Yaquis, and why Rufino did not go with us when we later left the village.

But I knew something that Beto did not know, even though I did not dream in the way that he did. I knew that what hadn't yet come for us lay just outside the village. I could not tell the shape of it, but I knew that it was large. It had no name that I knew. It was one of the new things brought by los vecinos, and it was part of a world that had no place for us. Perhaps that world had no name for us, either.

Every day the sun rose up and the shadows rolled back from the lips of the canyon, revealing the valley floor beneath, exposing it to the hot sun in a way that made the wheat and corn grow quickly, as though they were impatient to live and die.

But the people were changing in a way that I did not understand. The people in our village no longer seemed impatient to live, yet they feared dying. I did not understand how you could give up the will to live hard yet be afraid of death. It seemed to me that the old ways, the singing and dancing, the old cures, the old stories, were a way of holding off death, at least for a while.

The old people who remembered many things would go silent at the news of a stranger in the valley, refusing to open their lips on the ancient language, but not allowing the new language to pass from their mouths, either. As more and more strangers came to the valley, the old ones were mute more of the time, finally dying without the stories ever coming out of their mouths. In this way, I think, many things were lost, many stories were never told, and many songs were never sung.

I saw this happen, and it changed the way I saw my valley, the green fields and the stone buildings and the high canyon cliffs that had once offered comfort and shelter. Now I saw that it closed us in but could not keep the greater world out. I saw that and kept it in my heart, and so maybe I was not as hurt as the others when the time came to leave.

It was all we had ever known, that valley, the sun rising on one side and setting on the other. We knew the rhythm of work and the ache of cold and hunger, and we knew that we were part of all of it, the valley and the work and the abundance, and even the cold and the hunger. We were a part of the valley, and if we left it, we would change. I did not know if we would become a part of something else, that something waiting outside, or if we would die. Something inside told me that this is where we belonged, the sun rising on one side of the river and setting on the other, his wife, the moon, following behind. So even when the crops failed, even when the cotton would no longer grow and my people forgot that they had ever grown it, even when the Apaches came with their hard eyes and showed no more mercy than if our people had been insects, even then we stayed and buried the dead, and waited.

We did not know what we waited for, but I was determined

that I would not die no matter what came for us, soldier or priest or Apache. I knew that death had many faces but I had only one.

And so I began to ask questions about the outside, about the future, about myself.

✝

The Captains of War

And this is when my father told me about the great Opata leader, Refugio Tánori, who had come from a nearby village and was his uncle. My father's father and his uncle had been soldiers. Tánori had a vision that reached out of our valley and included the many valleys and plains and deserts around us, down to the water's edge, where the great ocean began that I had never seen.

A few years earlier, when the vecinos in Mexico did not want the vecinos in Spain to rule them anymore, the Dorame brothers, famous captains of war of the Opata, led an uprising of some of the Opata towns. The Dorames lived in Bacerac, and many people objected to the way the Opata were being treated by the new government. Already, soldiers were coming in and stealing land that was not theirs, land that was supposed to belong to the Opata for assisting the Spanish in fighting the Apache. Since the coming of the Spanish from their own country, the Opata had reached a truce with them and served in all-Opata units for their armies. But the new governors did not care.

The first war came in the 1820s, followed by a second a few years later. Many people were killed, both vecinos and Opata, ending in a major battle at Tónichi.

Under Dolores Gutiérrez, Opata troops then joined the Yaqui Juan Banderas in the 1830s to fight against the government of Sonora.

"We wanted our own country," said my father. "Until the Spaniards came, nobody owned anything like a country. God let us live on the land, and we took care of it. All we hoped was that the Aztecs would leave us alone and we could continue to trade with our cousins from the north.

"But after the Spaniards came, and after the Mexican government decided it could have its own country, we came to believe that we could have our own country, too. Una república de indios. The Country of Sonora. We had great dreams, but no arms.

"Then the French came and offered us hope. The French generals came to the Yaqui and Mayo and Opata chiefs and said, If you help us, we will give you your own land. You can have Sonora. It will be yours, and your people will not be separated from the land and made into slaves as the Spanish have done."

My father stopped and leaned on the stick he used for planting. His father had fought with Refugio Tánori in the next battles.

A little before I was born, my father said, Tánori had gotten together with the leaders from the other people, the Yaqui and the Mayo, and had a vision of a nation that was made up only of Indians, of the people like us who had lived on the land since before the white people, los vecinos, had arrived. It would be a place where we could farm and live in peace, safe from the soldiers, safe from the Mexican government, a place where we would make our own agreements and settle our differences in our own way, with our own courts. It was an idea that had been talked about for a long time, by both the captains of war and the captains of peace, the men who decided what a village would do under each circumstance.

It had remained just this, an idea, for a long time while the Yaqui fought with the Mexicans and the Opata tried to protect their land both from the marauding of the Apache and the tricks of the Mexicans who wanted to steal land from the Opata. But the Yaqui and the Opata had little in the way of weapons, only a few guns that they traded for or took from the Apache they killed, who got weapons from the North Americans.

Then the rich people of Mexico became tired of sending their wealth over the great ocean to Spain. They wanted to keep their wealth that they had stolen from the Indians, and wanted to have their own government. There was much fighting, and the Mexicans won, because Spain had soldiers all over the world and not enough to fight in Mexico. Mexico became free of Spain, and the captains of our people began to talk again, began to talk about what might be possible.

But not until the French came and wanted some of the land of Mexico did it seem possible.

And so, when the French landed at Guaymas, the Indians fought along with them. They fought against the Mexican generals and even fought against the Opatas who fought with the Mexicans. It was sad and bloody and did not turn out as the captains had hoped. Many people were killed, and the Mexicans threw the bodies of the Indians in the bay at Guaymas. The French were driven back, and Mexico remained its own country now, separate from Spain and France. But Sonora remained part of Mexico, full now of Mexican soldiers, who stole the land and gave it to the white people eager to settle in our river valleys and grow food for themselves.

The Opata general Refugio Tánori had led his men in support of the French-backed royalists. After a hard battle he was defeated at Mátape by Mexican troops who were also largely Opata. Tánori was executed, along with his brother.

"Now the Opata troops no longer fight together. The Mexicans do not trust us anymore."

My father shrugged and smiled and turned to go back to work. "And we do not trust them. We never should have trusted them in the first place."

The Mexican government made all of the Opata soldiers leave the army. The Opata had fought for the government since the first Spaniards had come, had helped them to defeat the Apache and secure the northern frontier, and had always been known for their bravery in battle. Generation after generation of Opata men had become soldiers and were proud of the good work they had done. They were paid by the government and so were able to give their families a little more food than could be grown or traded for.

Now the Opata soldiers were arrested or killed or told to go away from the army. There were no more units made up all of Opata soldiers because the new government was afraid of them, afraid of what the Opata remembered, and dreamed. Only those who said that they were not Opata could be in the army, and so there were no more units made up of only Opata, men who were related and could fight together as one.

All this my father told me, standing in his field that he farmed day after day, with sometimes me and sometimes my mother helping to plant the wheat and corn. My father was happy to farm and be with my mother. I do not think that he ever wanted to be a soldier, even though he was very proud of his father. He did not like it when we had to fight the Apaches, when they tried to raid our village and take our animals. Some of the men got very excited, their eyes got wide and they talked very rapidly, as if they were only truly alive when the Apaches came. They handled the guns as though they were lovers and talked about what they would do to an Apache if they caught one.

Once there had been captains of war and captains of peace. The captains of peace were the older men with much experience, and they held the courts and decided justice when there was a disagreement or something wrong had been done in the village. But now there were only captains of war, always younger men who were strong enough to fight. These were the men who stayed up all night before a battle, making themselves powerful with ritual. These were the men who went out once in a while to try and catch the Apache unaware.

My father only did this if he was asked. He never volunteered, and stayed quiet when the captains of war described their heroic feats. They would bring out the Apache scalps and talk about how hard they had fought to win them. The women even did the scalp dance once when I was little, but my father refused to be present. He said that some of us were Apache, which was true. The Opata used to save the children and raise them, if they found Apache children. The Apache did the same with our children. People in the village said that the Apache raided the towns as much for children as for livestock, because they were unable to have enough children.

My father said that the Apache were only a problem because the Spanish had given them horses, so they came out of the north, where they belonged. But some of the older men said the Apache had been fighting us even before then, and that is why the Opata were willing to cooperate with the Spanish. All I knew was that there had always been Apache and there had always been war. It was hard to imagine a time ruled by the captains of peace. More and more, the old people were silent.

In later years, I would miss my father very much. He was kind to me and made me laugh even when things were bad all around us.

In my valley, in the time before, young girls wore white dresses. When a girl became a woman, she began to wear a black skirt. Married women always wore their hair up. But an unmarried woman, even if she lived with a man and had children, wore her hair down. And she had pascola dancers at her funeral, just like a child. So did an unmarried man. That was the custom.

People were taken to the village of their birth for burial after the funeral. Sometimes it was very hard, for the body had to be carried a long way, sometimes to another valley. It is better to die close to home, close to the place where you were born.

In the time before, I was already in a dark skirt when the soldiers came. My sisters, only little girls of nine, were still in white dresses, and of course the baby, Beto, was, too. Only my brother Rufino was already a man.

The Yaquis had been having trouble for some time, but we had troubles of our own with the Apache. Not a month went by that someone did not lose cattle to the Apache, or a village was raided and people killed. We had a stone building in our village, very strong, and then there were places to put guns through and shoot. If there was time, everyone who could ran and got inside, and the door was shut tight. It was very scary. All the children cried.

This is not the way it used to be, my mother would say.

"This is not the way it used to be. This is not how it was in my village in the Sierras. We should return there, where it is safe. We are too close to the Americans and the Apaches here. We are better off with the Yaquis and the Mexicans."

But she was wrong.

My father would shrug and say nothing. He spent all day in the fields and was burnt dark by the sun. Only on feast days and Easter did he not work, because he was a pascola dancer. Only then did he change from a quiet man into a clown.

My little sisters were happy and pretty like my mother. I

was the quiet one, and although they didn't say it, I was the ugly one. I knew I was ugly, and it made me shy. I was tall and had big shoulders and big teeth. I looked like my father. But what made him handsome made me awkward.

My mother used to send me to bring water, because she knew I would come right back. If she sent the twins, they would stay by the spring and talk and talk. She only sent them when she wanted to know what was going on in town. Even my sisters, although they were little, made the boys look. They were so pretty, with small, dark features, just alike. They looked just like little dolls. My mother used to love to dress them up and braid white ribbons in their hair.

There was no spring nearby, only the river, so to get clean water, you had to find clean sand and dig a little hole. After a few minutes, when the hole filled up with water, you could dip your olla and fill it up. The sand made the water clean. This is what my mother taught me.

I used to be sad, once I started wearing a dark skirt, because I knew that the boys did not look at me. They turned and kept talking when I walked by carrying water by myself. If I was with the other girls, they would stop talking and pretend not to look, but we knew they were looking.

"Don't be sad," my father used to say. "You are tall and strong and you will have a husband someday."

Then he would tell me the story of the ugly woman who was visited by a devil. She was very sad because she thought she would never have a husband, never have someone to hold her.

"I could turn you into tobacco," said the devil. "Then men would always want you, always look for you, and they would hold you in their hands and stroke you."

The woman agreed. And that's how we came to have tobacco.

"I don't want to be tobacco," I would say. Then my father would laugh, and I would smile and start to feel better in spite of myself.

He used to say, "If you were tobacco, you could travel any-where in the world and see in the dark. You could be like a magic cigarette that witches use to spy on their enemies."

"But I don't want to travel," I would say. "I want to stay here with you." And he would laugh.

But that was a long time ago. Mostly my father was quiet. Like me. This was one of the stories my father told, when he was alive and we were happy in our village by the Moctezuma River. It was after this that the soldiers began to come and take men away. Women, too. They put people on trains going south and they were not seen again. It became difficult to go into Hermosillo or the bigger towns to trade, because the soldiers might stop you and put you on a train. There were families that disappeared overnight. One day they would have a house and land that they were farming, and then they would go to trade and never come back. People would wait awhile, then move into the houses or take over the fields. In some villages, vecinos moved into houses that had been owned by Indians. Everyone was hungry. What else was there to do?

Then it happened to us.

Rufino, at thirteen, was now the oldest male. No one men-tioned our father, but sometimes at night I could hear Chiri crying, muffling her sobs in her rebozo.

Father had been taken away by the soldiers. Because he was tall and strong like the Yaquis, he had been picked up in Hermosillo when he went there to buy seed corn. My mother's sister, Pancha, had seen them take him. She had followed and watched them put him on a train with many Yaqui and a few other Opata. Pancha's brother by marriage and nephew had gone, too.

Pancha was brave enough to ask a soldier where they were going. He was hungry and she had sold him some tortillas. He told her the men on the train would be taken to the capital and then to the Yucatán to cut hennequin for rope.

The men had only what they were carrying when they went to town. My father was still carrying the seed corn he had bought, but he threw the bag from the train to Pancha when it started to move. He could have kept it to eat, but he did not. The train, loaded down with Indians, pulled slowly away. Soldiers pointed rifles at the men so they would not try to jump.

Pancha gathered up the seed corn and came back to the village, crying. Her brother and nephew and brother-in-law were gone, as were most of the men of our village, either taken away or killed by soldiers.

In the villages farther north, the Apaches were fighting a battle to the death, but the Americans were fighting them, too, and the Apaches were losing. There were fewer and fewer of them, and the people of our village talked of going north to reclaim the old villages they had been driven from by the Apaches. In a drought, any puddle is wealth. At the time, this was all talk to me.

But when they came, when the soldiers came and took me by the arms and dragged me out from the pile of palm fronds where I had hidden, violating the hu'uki, violating the women's place, I felt myself falling, falling into a darkness, into a time before, where I could not be reached, where the hands touching me, pulling me, pulling at my clothes, could not reach me. I stayed in that darkness, not knowing for how long.

When I came back to myself, my mother was there, and other women from the village. We were outside near Pancha's house, which was now a smoking ruin.

"Drink this," my mother was saying. "Drink it all."

Chiri was pressing a cup to my lips. I took a swallow of the hot tea, then stopped. It tasted familiar, but much stronger and more bitter than I had ever tasted it before.

"Drink it all," Chiri repeated. "It will keep you from having a baby."

"A baby?" I asked.

I was confused. I tried to sit up but felt bruised and battered, as though I had fallen off a trail and rolled down the side of the mountain.

"I'm going to have a baby?" I was heavy and sore, and felt as though a great weight pressed upon me. "But I haven't talked to anyone."

No one answered me, but Chiri continued to press the cup to my lips and made me drink the hot, bitter tea until it was all gone. Then I curled up and fell into a deep, dreamless sleep.

†

Javier Oposura

After our father was taken away with the Yaqui, we waited and waited for him to return, or for a letter to arrive. There was nothing. My mother went twice to Hermosillo with her sister to ask the authorities about him, but she did not know anybody there, and she did not speak Spanish. Some said all the Yaqui men had been sent south, far away. Others said they had been taken to Guaymas and thrown in the bay. We never heard from my father again. I missed him a lot, and cried, because he had been good to me. He liked me even though I was ugly, because I looked like him.

We did not plant the milpas that year, because we had no man to do it. My mother did not want to do it by herself, and everyone else in the village was working as hard as they could. Although Rufino was fourteen, he would not do it by himself, saying he did not know how. He and my mother fought all the time. He was now the man of the house and should have taken care of us, but instead he left and went to live with our cousins. My brother liked to drink mescal and did not like to work.

That winter we had nothing to eat but beans and tortillas and pinole without sugar. We even ate the seed corn. The girls were hungry all the time and cried for food. Even little Beto, although he still nursed, got a bad cough that kept us awake night after night. My mother and I made many baskets and petates to sell, but we didn't have money for anything but a few beans. I felt very faint all the time because I was giving most of my food to my sisters. I would move in a haze to the river, barely able to lift the full olla of water to my head to carry it back.

One day in early spring, coming back from the water hole, I saw my mother talking to El Gusano. My stomach lurched, and I stepped into a doorway so she would not see me. They were talking quietly, the way El Gusano would talk with a man. I could not believe it. Maybe she is finding a way to get food, I thought. Maybe he will bring us food from outside. All winter I had thought of nothing but canned peaches. I had them once at a fiesta and they were the sweetest thing I had ever eaten. That winter I woke up every morning wishing for canned peaches.

El Gusano came back about a month later. I did not say anything, but I watched my mother. She would not look at me. Nothing bad happened then, but nothing good, either. I decided she had been trying to get more food for us.

About this time Javier Oposura came to our village. He had known my father and been in Hermosillo when my father was taken away.

As soon as my mother heard that Javier Oposura was there, she took the olla and went to get water. She came back with Javier. He came to tell us what happened, she said, and brought us food, so we were very happy to see him. But he did not know any more than Pancha, and had only heard from others what had happened. Then he stayed around. He did not go back to his village, wherever it was, or to his wife and children. He started to stay with us in our house.

Only once had I seen my mother get water, and that was the day she met Javier Oposura. I saw it. And although I did not understand at the time, I remembered it after everything else happened.

Javier was a famous Apache-fighter—his name meant Javier Fierce-Hearted in our language. He had gone on many raids into the Sierras chasing Apaches, and killed many of them. He also loved to sing and tell stories and was a popular card-player. If El Gusano was in town, or had just visited and there was plenty of mescal or tesquino to drink, the men would play cards and tell stories for many hours. Some of the children used to listen, but I was too shy to stay close, especially when I was older. My mother would not have approved. But maybe I would have paid more attention if I had known what would happen.

Javier lived in a village near ours, and sometimes he would pass through on horseback on one of his adventures. He was said to have an Opata wife and many children.

He wasn't tall, but he was strong. He had relatives among the Tarahumara, and came and went across the mountains as though they were nothing. No one I knew had ever been across the mountains to the east, where there was said to be a great city, Chihuahua, full of horses and carriages and buildings as big as mountains.

His mother's family lived on the other side of these mountains and went into Chihuahua to trade. Javier wore a long mustache and dressed like a Mexican but he spoke Opata and Tarahumara.

It was during these hard times that we heard about El Tecolote. It was when we had nothing—no livestock, no crops and nothing to eat. One morning a few weeks after Javier Oposura came, my mother said, "Bring some of your things and your sisters' things. We are going to see this Tecolote. Maybe he can help us."

Many people from our village left to see El Tecolote. As we walked north, more and more people joined us. Like a great movement of wind or weather, we moved north and east against the mountains, towards the Apache, through the canyons and cuts and waterways, where we saw the earthworks of the ancients. We went to hear the words of the healer who came to visit for a while.

At each step of the way the old people said, This was ours. Our people lived here and built this, they farmed these barrancas and made these old stone buildings. They were a great people who came down from the North. This was once ours. The Tarahumara looked at us from their lofty houses and the Apaches stood on their patient ponies and watched us pass but did not attack. Even they saw that this was something holy.

And at each crossing, each place where valleys came together or roads merged, we came across more people swept up in the tide of faith. Some carried the very old or infirm. Others came as though fulfilling a manda, dragging a cross or walking on their knees. All spoke of El Tecolote as though they had waited for him all of their lives. He was the messenger, the one whose voice meant death for the enemy.

I was in wonder at all of this. I had never been out of my village or seen so many people from different places. The way they talked and dressed was strange to me, and I did not understand much of it. But I think I knew even then that I would never see my village again.

I traveled with my mother. I carried my brother Beto much of the way while Chiri helped my twin sisters. We traveled with Javier Oposura, who had come to live with my mother after our father was taken away on the train.

And this is what happened. We waited the better part of a day at a crossroads, where one way led east into the mountains towards Casas Grandes, and one way led west into the desert. I did not understand why we were waiting, and could see that Javier Oposura was impatient. All day people passed us by, walking east to see El Tecolote.

Early in the afternoon a man I recognized came up to us. He greeted my mother and Javier Oposura, his hat pulled low over his eyes. He looked quickly at me and my sisters but said nothing to us. It was El Gusano. He and my mother and Javier Oposura walked a little ways away from us and began to talk. Every once in a while El Gusano would look over at us. I began to have a bad feeling.

At one point I heard my mother say, "No. No más la una," only the one.

Then they talked some more, until I saw my mother agreeing to something, Javier assuring her that it was all right. But I did not feel that it was all right. Beto was hungry and fussy, and I jiggled him on my back as they talked and talked.

And then the most terrible thing of my life happened, the thing that I will never forget. My mother took Beto from my arms and gestured towards El Gusano with her eyes.

"You go with him now," she said mildly. "You and the girls. He will take you to a new place."

"We are not going with you?" I cried.

"It is very dangerous where we are going. But if we make it, we can stay with Javier's mother's people."

I stood rooted to the ground like a stump. I did not know what to say. But in that moment, my sisters looking with dark troubled eyes between me and my mother, a piece of my heart broke off and died. My mother would not look at us. She busied herself with settling Beto on her back. Javier Oposura looked impatient as others continued to pass us and take the trail into the mountains. He had been leading a horse all of this time. Now he mounted and helped my mother with Beto up behind.

Only El Gusano and me and my sisters were left standing there in the road.

"Mamá!" cried Segua suddenly. "Are we to be married?"

My mother turned slowly, letting go of Javier's waist. She focused on El Gusano, who stood without speaking a word all this time, as he often did while others sorted things out around him.

"Yes," she said. "You will go to Tucson and be married." She did not look at us or take her eyes off El Gusano.

"When will we see you?" I asked, my heart sinking fast, tears like rain starting down my face.

"When God wills it," she said. "Que se vayan con Dios." And she turned away.

We cried and cried. I tried to hug little Beto, for I had taken care of him the most, as much as my mother. He did not understand, but he cried, too.

I tried to hide my face, but my mother made me stand up straight.

"Do not be ashamed," she said. "Do not be scared. Where we are going, we may die."

My mother could not have dreamed of the things that happened to us when we went away from our village, of the pain we would suffer, of the strange houses we would walk in. We had been taught all of our lives not to talk to strangers, or even people who were not our relatives unless our mother was present, and now she cast us out into a world of strangers who cared no more for our ways than for the dust beneath their feet.

We walked a long way with El Gusano, farther than I had ever been. Pretty soon we came to a road that wagons could go on. There, a man with a wagon and a horse met us and we got in.

With nothing to eat, we rode away. The twins said nothing, nothing, as though they had known it would happen all along, that our father would not return and we would have to leave our home and everything we knew behind. Even when, a few miles down the road, the men stopped the wagon and took the twins and went behind some trees, they said nothing. Even when they came back with their eyes and lips puffy and their hands shaking, their dresses torn, they just looked at me with their jet-black eyes and said nothing.

After two days, we came out onto the open desert. We were heading north. Neither El Gusano or the other man had spoken to us since we had gone with them. It was almost June, the fiesta of San Juan. This had once been a time of much rejoicing in our village, with contests between the young men to show who was the best on horseback. They would try to pull a rooster from the ground that had been buried up to his neck. It was when the rains came and everyone was happy.

And then it rained. The heavens opened up and water came gushing from the sky in an uninterrupted torrent. No one could see or hear. We crouched in the back of the wagon while the men ran about searching, futilely, for cover.

The rain covered everything, soaked into it, possessed it, submerged it. The rain became all-encompassing, all-knowing. Thunder boomed and rolled across the sky. The men ran. My sisters and I jumped out of the wagon and pressed ourselves in between some rocks. The horse screamed and bolted with the wagon.

Then the lightning came. It struck without mercy, incinerating trees and bushes, cracking boulders, scouring what was left of the landscape.

The air had a strange, sharp smell. The lightning struck again and again, until we did not know if we were alive or dead. We lay upon the ground, blind, deaf, at the mercy of the desert and its guardians.

When the storm had passed, the desert was silent. I raised my head to see if I could find my sisters. I saw them across the way, looking at me. They were saying something, but I could not hear them. I lay for a few minutes more, listening to the pounding silence, watching for the men, wary of showing myself from the depression where I lay. I was not sure if it had been there before or if the waters had carved it out around me.

Then one of my sisters pointed at her ear, where I saw blood running out, and I decided that she could not hear, either.

The stranger came back from wherever he had run. El Gusano was nowhere to be found. We could not hear the man, although his lips were moving. He searched some more. There was a smell like burnt meat. Then the man found El Gusano. He was dead. The lightning had killed him. The man took El Gusano by the arms and dragged him into some bushes. He did not even bother to bury him. The stranger was angry. He made us get up and walk with him. Eventually we caught up with the horse, but the wagon was damaged, broken up from the horse's running through the rocks.

We camped where we were that night, in the middle of nothing. For the first time the man gave us some food from sacks that had been in the wagon. He built a fire and we tried to dry out our clothes.

The next day, the man stood and smoked his wet tobacco. He looked at us, then looked at the skinny horse. He put my two sisters up on it and got up himself. Then he looked at me and rode away. I waited awhile, but they did not come back.

I began to walk.

Day into night, night into day. One day bleeds seamlessly into the next, one moon into the other, rabbit of the moon running, always running. I was beginning to see things, to have things in front of my eyes that were not really there. I kept trying to brush them away, like cobwebs. I was very scared, but I could not show it to my sisters. Although part of me knew that I was alone, I tried not to think about it, so I kept thinking of my sisters, that I would catch up to them very soon and take care of them, get them away from this man.

I tried not to think about El Gusano lying back there in the desert. The spirit of a person killed by lightning can stay there for days. I tried not to think that his spirit was left to wander alone, that he might come this way looking for the man who had left him unburied.

Stay close to water, my mother had said. If I stayed close to water, following the source of each stream and river, la corúa, the great snake, would protect me. La corúa was a being from the old times, she told me in the hu'uki, from before the Spanish came and tried to change everything. La corúa was the rainbow, the bridge across the sky between God and the people. He was a great snake who slept in a cave near the source of the river and would protect those who called upon him as he protected the water. If he was killed, the water would dry up and the people who lived there would die or have to move away.

But when I got to Tucson, I could not find anyplace to offer thanks to la corúa, only shrines to the Catholic saints, to the inocentes and the dead. By now, there were many dead and we had much to pray for. Perhaps la corúa is dead, too, I thought. Maybe he went away when the soldiers came or maybe they killed him when they killed our people.

The Papago in Tucson talk about I'itoi, their creator, but that is different. I'itoi lives in a cave on the east side of a big mountain and he was still alive. But there is only one I'itoi, and he belongs to the Papago. Each river, on the other hand, had its corúa, its protector, who gave water to all who came, Opata, Yaqui, Papago, Pima, or vecino. He brought rain, sometimes too much at once, and he always lived by the water. It is where the saying came from when it rained a lot, una media culebra de agua.

These things were too much for me to understand. They were the place of great maestros and captains of peace and curanderos. All I really knew was work.

My feet were polished by the sand, my soles like ironwood from walking across the hot, rocky ground. My hair was bleached red from the sun, the ends ragged and dry, and my skin burnished like metal.

I walked a long way, and many things happened that I do not remember. I went through villages where people gave me food and told me the way to Tucson. I saw places where people did not live anymore, the fruit trees gone wild, the houses empty. I learned to walk a long way without water to drink. I learned to eat whatever there was to eat.

When men came on horses, I flattened myself against the ground and hid until the strangers were gone, pressing myself hard into the sharp rocks and thorns so as to seem part of them. After a while, I felt that I really was a part of them—no longer human or part of a village, but just another part of the desert. I did not think, I did not feel. I just walked.

La Plancha

A duras penas, when I arrived in Tucson I had no one. I had not eaten more than the roots of the earth in days, and I had no place to stay. The men terrified me. The women terrified me. I hid under a big bush near the road where people came and went all day until an old toothless woman came up and said, "Oye, si quieres comer, hay trabajo"—if you want to eat, there is work.

I came out from under my bush. My face was dirty and my hair was full of weeds and brambles. Brushing myself off as best as I could, I followed the old woman, who led me, cackling and beckoning, to a shack closer to town.

Sitting in front of the shack—which had a large, locked padlock on it—was a woman who I came to know was called La Plancha. From her left side, she looked perfectly normal, but when she looked right at you, you could see that her face was horribly disfigured. I wondered what had happened to her.

One side of La Plancha's face was a livid scar from her chin to above her right eye, where the scar came to a point, the point of the iron. A portion of her eye could just open from the inside corner. The eyebrow was completely obliterated, along with La Plancha's former name and identity.

La Plancha gave advice on jobs to the other Indians, for she often knew when employers were looking for laborers or domestic help, and had a knack for finding the right person to fill the job.

A rancher, store owner, brothel keeper, or servant would come to La Plancha where she sat in front of her locked shack, maybe bring her some cigarettes or whiskey, and describe the position to her. La Plancha would choose among the many people who came to see her daily and send the appropriate person or family on to that position. In return, the person turned over a portion of his or her earnings to La Plancha, at least for a month or two, enabling her to keep body and soul together.

La Plancha had heard there was a girl under a bush and guessed that I had just arrived from the interior.

By the time I emerged, terrified and light-headed with starvation, I did not really care what happened to me. I did not know where my sisters were or how to begin to find them. My family was scattered. I was not sure at that time that I should even be alive.

But La Plancha looked at me for a long time, as though measuring me for a dress.

"Where do you come from?" she asked.

"El Arbolito," I answered. "I left with my two sisters when there was no food left. Our mother sent us." I left out the part about El Gusano.

"Where are your sisters?" she asked.

I could not look at her. "Probably dead."

I felt La Plancha scrutinize me with first her good eye, then her bad. She smoked and said nothing for a long time.

I did not know what to do and finally sat down on the ground, too weak to stand any longer.

"You have an honest face," La Plancha finally said. "There is a family on the south side of town, a good barrio, looking for a girl."

I stood up. I could not tell how old La Plancha was, but she spoke with authority.

"They are called Moreno. This vieja, Juana, will show you the way."

As I began to walk away, she called out to me, "What do they call you?"

"Shark's Tooth," I answered.

La Plancha shook her head. "No es nombre cristiano," she said. "From now on, you are Concha."

Juana laughed at La Plancha, showing two or three teeth, and asked what good it was to her. La Plancha tossed her a coin, which Juana caught in one fist and buried in the folds of her clothing. Without looking back, Juana started off for town, and I realized I was to follow.

Juana talked as we walked along. She guessed my first question. La Plancha, it was said, had worked as a maid for a rich family. Some jewelry had gone missing and she was accused of the crime. La Plancha was ironing a big pile of clothing at the time. When she insisted that she was innocent, the family held her down while the aggrieved wife put the hot iron to her face, scarring and marking her forever. Then she was let go.

We walked and walked, first past the jacales of the Indians, far apart, separated by milpas and cactus fences, the river close by on our left. Then we turned away from the river, and a few dirt tracks began to appear where the houses stood closer together. I concentrated on my feet, putting one in front of the other. I had lost my sandals long ago, and now my feet were like stone. But my head was like cotton—drifting, drifting.

Finally we came to stop in front of a big plain house. There were a couple of outbuildings in back, and a big cottonwood shaded the front of the house, which faced west, towards the river and the Santa Catalina Mountains beyond, now about half a mile to our left.

Juana made a whooping noise that scared me, then ran off. I stood rooted to the ground in front of the house.

A woman in an apron opened the door and saw me standing out there.

"¿Bueno?" she said.

"La Plancha," I managed to force out.

"La Plancha sent you? Qué bueno."

The woman motioned for me to follow her around the side of the house to the back, where she was cooking over a woodstove.

"What is your name?" asked the woman.

My head felt like birds, like air. "Concha," I said, feeling the word in my mouth for the first time. "I am called Concha."

I did not know whether or not to trust these people. I had never been around people who were not from my own village, and had been brought up never to speak with strangers. I kept my eyes on the ground as Mrs. Moreno spoke to me, telling me where things were, having me give greens to the goat they kept for milk. She used many words that I did not know.

"¿Entiendes?" she kept asking. I just nodded.

If they serve peaches, I told myself, then I will stay. I helped Mrs. Moreno set out food. It was as much food as I could remember seeing all at once for a single family. Once, long ago, the people of El Arbolito had given big fiestas with lots of food, but that seemed like a dream now.

When I saw them dishing out a big can of peaches, I realized that I had been sent to these people by God. He had heard my prayer. I stayed and had supper behind the house that night after everyone else had been served, listening to their conversation inside. This is how I learned more Spanish, by listening to other people talk to each other.

Mrs. Moreno said that I could sleep in the cooking ramada. She did not ask if I had any other place to go.

The next day, the Señora filled the big tin with water and let me take a bath. I had never sat in a little tin to bathe but had always swum in the river. Then she gave me a new dress.

She asked me to stay and help with the house. I could clean and take care of the children, she said.

"Do you know how to take care of children?" she asked.

"Yes," I said, "I am the oldest of my family."

There were three children, all young, and I soon realized that Mrs. Moreno was expecting a fourth. She did not dress differently, the way women in my village did when expecting a baby. Mrs. Moreno dressed like the other women in Tucson, except her clothes were looser. I missed my brothers and sisters but did not think about it too hard. It made me happy to be able to feed Mrs. Moreno's babies with good food, to dress them in their little clothes and see them smile.

The food was very good, almost too good, for Señor Moreno was a partner in a carnecería on South Meyer. He brought home the parts that did not sell, and the family ate tripas y chorizo, great stews of beef and goat scraps. At first the food was too rich for me, and I had to eat beans and rice, taking just a little of the meat. I learned to make cheese from the goat's milk, and tried not to turn away in disgust from the bloody smell of Mr. Moreno when he returned from a long day at work.

Fortunately, once a week an old Yaqui woman came and took their wash away to the river and brought it back cleaned and ironed.

They gave me some blankets and Mr. Moreno even built a little table and put it outside of the ramada where I could sew or play with the children. I was very happy. I had never slept in a house with a floor before. I had been grateful for the stone wall at the back of my old home. It made me sad to think of El Arbolito, my father and mother gone, not knowing what had become of my sisters.

Mrs. Moreno sometimes asked me about my family. All I said was that the Apaches had made everyone leave. And my father had been taken away with the Yaqui men. This part made the Señora very sad and she would begin to cry. They were familiar with the Moctezuma River of Sonora, because Mr. Moreno had traveled more before he had married and decided it was unsafe. He had worked for one of the freight companies that delivered goods up and down the river valleys. They did not know my father, but they knew my people.

There was no food, I told them, so I had come north with my sisters. We walked a very long way and had been very hungry and thirsty. We became separated, and I did not know what happened to them. This is all I felt I could say. I did not know if they were alive or dead, and this part made me very sad.

At first, the Morenos did not believe I had walked so far. But I told them the names of the places I had been, the way that I had traveled, and they believed me. They knew where my village was and that the Apache had gotten very bad.

"It's a miracle that you are alive," Señora Moreno would say.

Yes, I would think. I would remember the canned peaches and think *that* was the miracle—finding these people. I could be starving on the street, or worse.

The Morenos knew many people, and once there was a visit planned from a prominent family in Tucson, an Anglo family. They would be coming over after Mass on Sunday. The Anglo family attended Mass at Holy Family, while the Morenos prayed at San Augustín. Mrs. Moreno aired out the parlor, knowing that they would be sensitive to the pervasive smell of menudo that had boiled in the adjacent ramada all the day before.

"A smell that is good to us," she told me, "is bad to them."

She insisted that I put on a clean dress and had my hair neat.

The mother and her grown son sat in the parlor, where I brought them iced tea and pecan cookies the way that Mrs. Moreno had taught me, offering first one and then the other.

Mrs. Vaughan was a great, stout woman dressed in black finery. She was in permanent mourning since the death of her husband, I understood from their conversation, but on her the black looked defiant, like armor against the world. The late Mister Vaughan had invested in mining ventures in Sonora and now the widow Vaughan ran his business. The mother and son picked at the food I offered them.

Mr. Moreno had worked for Mister Vaughan at some point, supplying one of his mines. He jumped up to grab a plate that was about to slip from Mrs. Vaughan's hand, then apologized for his sudden movement. I had never seen the Morenos behave this way before.

The Morenos, I realized later, treated Mrs. Vaughan and her son the way they treated all the Anglos, with exaggerated politeness and the frequent repetition of simple, soothing phrases, as though they were in need of constant reassurance and comforting words.

Mrs. Vaughan sat in the best chair and seemed to preside over the afternoon, although she was only the guest. She overwhelmed the parlor with her great size.

I had never seen anyone who looked like the son. In spite of the things that I had learned from my own mother and by watching how people behaved in Tucson, I could not keep myself from staring at him. The son had flaming hair and pale blue eyes that seemed unprotected, unnatural, as though placed temporarily in his face. He sat in a chair too low for him, his knees jutting upward, and fiddled with his hat. He did not talk much.

Mrs. Vaughan told the Morenos that her son did not apply himself to the family enterprises, never took an interest in the affairs that she now managed without her husband. He was out at all hours of the day and night with disreputable characters, she said. Mrs. Vaughan spoke as though her son was not there, or was deaf. I wondered if he could see normally, or was impaired in some other way besides his looks. Perhaps, the way his mother talked about him, he was simple.

He reminded me of a mule that was about to kick, his pale eyes rolling in his head, and I ducked my head when he looked at me. I was relieved when they left and the Morenos returned to their regular selves again.

✝

Train

For days the family had talked of nothing else. The neighbors stood in front of their houses, the men gathered along Meyer and Congress, the women called to each other across their fences of dry posts and ocatilla. You would have thought that it was the most important thing in the world, that it was about to change their lives forever. Most people planned to go out and see it arrive.

This was not too long after I had come to live with the Morenos. I was beginning to understand more—where to get water, how to cook food the way the family liked it, not to question the waste of water on plants that gave no food in Mrs. Moreno's garden. I had learned to answer Mr. Moreno when he spoke to me, although he was not a relative of mine. I still could not look directly at him, and waited for the words of disapproval that never came because my mother and the other women were not there to correct my behavior.

But I loved the children and sang them the songs and played the clapping games with them that I had learned at home. They were not allowed out in the street unless I went with them, so they took me to the store or down the street to a fountain, sometimes, to play. In this way I learned a little about the streets near the house and saw how people dressed and acted in Tucson.

The children insisted that I go with the family on this outing, and the Morenos had no objection. Mrs. Moreno even loaned me a hat for the occasion and showed me how to put my hair up on my head.

"You look more . . . refined that way," said Mrs. Moreno.

The hat could not cover my hair, however, so it sat on top of my head, held on by a long black ribbon. People streamed from every corner of the city, on foot, on horseback or in carriages. The women were dressed in their finest and the men wore hats and ties as though going to church. The children in their uniforms were out of school, the girls holding bunches of flowers and the boys waving flags. I had never seen so many people in my life.

As we stood in the sweltering sun, lined up along two lengths of metal that ran along a rocky road, I thought I heard a familiar sound. At first I could not believe my ears, for I had been told that they were all tame in Tucson, that they had been settled into a barrio and no longered bothered people. But when I heard it again, there could be no mistake. The Apaches were attacking, and we were out in the open with no place to run. In panic, I felt myself falling, falling into the street, falling into a deep blackness that shut everything else out, knowing that I would not survive this time.

I lay in darkness for a long time. I swam in the cool depths of the river, the fish playing about my feet, my long hair wrapped about me. I could hear the other girls drumming the water above me, a sound we made by cupping our hands together and striking the surface of the water. Their voices ebbed and flowed around me. When I came to the surface, I was lying by the side of the iron road, the children jumping all around. Mrs. Moreno was fanning me with the hat. Somewhere, a band was playing loud military music.

"You missed it, you missed it!" screamed Josefina. "Come on! We'll never get a chance to see it if you don't get up."

Mr. Moreno had already gone ahead, leaving Mrs. Moreno and the children behind with me. The first train had arrived in Tucson, and he wasn't about to miss the ceremonies.

Through much explanation as we walked, I was told that the train was many coaches linked together that moved without a horse. I finally saw the huge thing, chuffing and sweating like a bull. Then there was that horrible noise again, and I covered my ears in terror. But no one else seemed to mind. They all stood where they were and looked very pleased. The sound had come out of the train.

And yes, there were Apaches there, but they were Apaches mansos, the tame Apaches, who had been persuaded to put on their ceremonial regalia and stand meekly to the side while the men in black suits talked and talked. I decided that these must be the captains of the town. I kept an eye on the Apaches. But as I looked at them, I could see red eyes, flaccid muscles, and unhealthy skin under their garish war paint. One of the men swayed and staggered and finally sat down on the ground. The others appeared not to notice. These were indeed Apaches mansos, sunk into a stupor of liquor and inactivity. They were no threat to me. And I felt a little better. I may have nothing, I thought, but at least I am strong and healthy.

I thought it was a strange time of day for all of these people to be standing out in the sun, not working, not dancing, not trading or making a fiesta, just standing there listening to these men say incomprehensible things about the future of Tucson and the good of the people. In my village, such a meeting would have begun at dusk and lasted through the night. The children fidgeted and the flags and flowers began to droop. The Apache manso sitting on the ground was soon fast asleep. I was happy when it was over and I could return to the comfort of the ramada.

I grew used to the screams of the train which came more and more often as time went on, and came to see that they brought new things to the stores that Mrs. Moreno wanted to buy. Mr. Moreno talked about how fortunate he was that he had gotten out of the transport business, because the train would take customers away from the stagecoach lines and soon put them out of business. It took a lot of money to run a train, and was not something that a couple of men with a few dollars and a lot of ganas, as he said, could start for themselves.

Mr. Moreno used words like *business* and *government* a lot, and used them as though he was talking about something a lot larger than several older men holding council. He used them as though they were as important to him as whether or not it would rain, or if there was enough food to last until the next planting season. Within a year or two, what he said came true— the stagecoaches went out of business. I did not know where the train came from or where it went. I asked if it went to my village, Los Arbolitos, but no one seemed to know. They said Porfirio Díaz was building railroads that would soon make Mexico a modern country.

But as often as I heard the train whistle, the sound of it late at night made me wrap a blanket tight around myself and watch the dark outside. I thought about the nights spent in the stone building the village used as a fortress—the men tense at the windows, holding the two guns they owned, stumbling over the goats and smaller children in the dark, the babies crying as the grown-ups strained to interpret the noises in the smoke and confusion outside.

The adults had taken turns holding vigil, and sometimes

my mother, Chiri, held one of the guns because she was a good shot. She was a good horse rider, too, and had once made all of the men in the village angry by riding out in the middle of a rooster pull and plucking the bird out from under the horse's hooves of the young man who was expected to win. I couldn't help it, she said afterwards. I just had to try it once to see if it was so hard.

But when it came to fighting the Apaches, they did not mind that my mother liked to shoot. The Opata had always treated their women with respect, and the Mexicano way of telling women what to do came slowly to our village, since there were no Mexican families living with us at that time. The women owned the land and had once had their own societies, and the old people told stories of how brave the women had been fighting the Spanish soldiers when they first came to Sonora.

We had once spent four days holding off a large raiding party of Apaches, fainting from the lack of air and water in our room like a prison, while the Apaches looted and burned the village below. Rafaela, the woman who lived across the river, had been killed that time. There had not been time for her to get to the stone building on the cliff. Her children had been killed or stolen. All the cattle had been run off, and several families had taken what they could carry and moved away forever after that. I wondered where they were now, and if they were as lonely for home as I was, listening to that whistle scream in the dark.

Barrio Libre

When I found my sisters, they were called Lucy and Flora. I was walking down a street I had never seen before when I was startled by a woman with paint on her face putting a hand on my shoulder.

When I recovered from my susto, I said, "You look like a Pima!" and hugged my little sister for the first time in two years. "I can't believe that you are alive!"

"I can't either," said Lucy. "You can't imagine. Any of it. Not any of it. Come see where we live."

It was a big house. The patio was set up like a hotel with potted plants and big wicker chairs where men sat drinking. All of them stared at us when we walked in and I did not like it. There was a wrought-iron stairway at the back. My sisters shared a cubicle upstairs.

"They like to dress us like children," said Flora, who had been sleeping.

"You are children," I said, "just unmarried girls."

"It doesn't matter anymore," said Flora. "No one will want

us now. Besides, we get paid. In gold."

Flora showed me their savings wrapped in a real silk stocking. I could not tell what it was worth, but it seemed like a lot.

I told them about the Morenos. "They treat me well. I take care of the children and help cook. It is a lot of work, but there is plenty of food."

There was a cook at the house where my sisters lived. They said all the men who came to the house were norteamericanos.

Neither of them had heard from my mother.

I went back downstairs with Lucy, where a man stood by the door smoking.

"Mr. Dibbett, this is my sister Concha."

Mr. Dibbett put his hand on my chin and turned my face to look at it. I did not like this.

"Not bad, but not very friendly," he said, looking away from me. "A little big through the shoulders," he added.

"She's not for you," said Lucy, and moved his hand away from my face. "I am." She stood close to him so that he put his arm around her. "Mr. Dibbett is going to marry me and take me away from here."

Mr. Dibbett said nothing.

I did not know why, but I felt like crying. My sisters were alive. They did not need me. I moved to go out.

"Tell us if you need anything," called Lucy.

I shut the door behind me, then pulled the rebozo well over my head and face lest anyone see me walking out of that house, out of that street, out of the scandalous Barrio Libre.

The Weeping Pearls

Concha was sometimes alone in the house, if the family went visiting or made a special visit to Carrillo's Gardens, a place of flowers, music, and earthly delights that had been constructed close to Tucson by the resourceful Leopoldo Carrillo. Always mindful of a dollar, Señor Carrillo had purchased some land near a natural spring and combined his two great loves: gardening and money. It was a popular source of family entertainments, and close to the Mexican part of town.

During these periods of solitude, Concha was able to study the objects in the house at her own leisure — to turn over the wind-up clock, look under the rugs, and especially, to look at the wonderful beds that were up off of the floor and dressed in their own clothes. Many people in Sonora had beds, but they were constructed of poles lashed together with a rawhide stretched across them and secured around the edges. These were altogether different, with sturdy flat feet and mattresses that made them seem more like soft tables.

One day the Morenos came home unexpectedly from a visit

to Carrillo's Gardens. Concha was standing in their bedroom with Mrs. Moreno's pearls in her hands, examining the little round globules that looked like frozen water. Mrs. Moreno had told her once that they came all the way from China, where a fish had made them in its shell. Concha held them up to the light, wondering if she could see through them, but she could not. She ran her thumb over the smooth, almost oily surfaces, wondering why a fish would need such a thing. Concha had never seen the sea, and wondered at a place so vast that whole countries could float in it without being seen from Tucson.

Concha, afraid they would think she was stealing the pearls and that she would end up looking like La Plancha, scrambled beneath the bed. To her further horror, Mr. and Mrs. Moreno made straight for the bedroom, shut the one door within the house, and began to take off their clothes.

Concha was awestruck. While she knew that her parents had done this, it must have been furtive and silent, or out in the fields. By contrast, Mr. Moreno spoke in a low voice to Mrs. Moreno, who responded with little sighs and giggles. Curled beneath the bed, the necklace clasped to her lips, her heart pounding in her throat, Concha felt like the cricket who witnessed the conception of the world as the sun and the moon made love in the bed/sky above her. She hardly breathed until they were done. After they had dressed and re-emerged into the world, Concha was able to replace the pearls and slip out the back door to her customary place in the ramada behind the cooking shed.

One stifling afternoon the Señora fell asleep in the parlor while waiting for her husband to return from an errand so they could attend a fiesta. She dozed off briefly and had dreams of people and places she did not recognize. She saw them running, running desperately to a place where they thought they would be safe, slamming a heavy door behind them, barracading it against the Apaches. She awoke with a start and felt the pearls tingling against her skin. She touched them with her fingertips, groggy in the afternoon heat. Returning to her room, the Señora removed the pearls and replaced them with another necklace.

After that, she would take the pearls out of their red, silken drawstring pouch in preparation for going out, but found herself putting them away before choosing something else.

When Concha disappeared, the Morenos searched the house to see if anything had been taken. At Mr. Moreno's suggestion, the Señora opened her jewelry case and saw that the silken bag containing her pearls was dark with moisture. She looked gingerly inside, expecting to see them gone. But no, the pearls were there, damp and glistening like tears, smelling faintly of the sea. She quickly searched through her other jewels and precious belongings but could find nothing missing. Only the pearls seemed disturbed, and continued to bead up with moisture even as Mrs. Moreno wiped them clean. Only then did the Señora feel that something was terribly wrong.

When it happened to Concha, she did not feel like the cricket. She did not feel like the sun, or even like the moon. She knew that it was not like that between the Morenos, or even for her sisters who were paid money for it. Maybe the first time, when they were little.

Even knowing what had happened to them, she had not imagined the pain and humiliation, the burning shame that went with it. It took what seemed a long time to Concha. She felt his utter contempt for her, his feeling that he could get what he wanted because of who he was, who his father had been, and because of who she wasn't.

When George Vaughan stood over her buttoning his pants, a look of complete smugness and satisfaction on his face in spite of the scratch marks she had left there, Concha felt hate for the first time in her life.

Blood trickling from the side of her mouth where he had struck her, Concha reached up the wall against which she lay. Without taking her eyes off of George, she reached up and grasped the lace skirt on the Virgin of Guadalupe standing quietly in her niche and gathered the holy ankles into her hands. With all her strength, Concha rose to her feet and swung the plaster statue down on George's head just as he turned away. Had he not turned, she might have killed him. As it was, she struck a blow to the side of his head that sent him staggering, clutching at his flaming hair as a darker red welled up within it.

George grabbed his hat and ran, never looking again at Concha. It was as though she wasn't even there.

Concha fled, too. She ran blindly, not knowing where she was going or what she was doing, leaving a trail of blood on the dusty ground. She ran all the way back to where the Papago lived south of town. When she got there, she realized that she was looking for the bush under which she had lived for three days when she first arrived in Tucson. She stood in the road, looking wildly about her, blood dripping from her lip and running down her legs. Her dress was torn. The Papago women, upon seeing her face, gathered Concha inside and began boiling herbs to cure her susto.

Nothing seemed to help. Concha shivered and cried out and could not sleep. She screamed and rolled her eyes and would not be left alone, even for a moment. Although they tried to clean her and see to her wounds, Concha did not want to be touched, and it was several days before she collapsed in exhaustion and allowed herself to be bathed.

No one knew what had happened to her, although they had a pretty good idea.

After many days, the susto did not abate. Finally, a famous curandera from Sonora was sent for. She stood looking at the trembling girl crouched in a corner. Concha had not eaten since she had been found. Her eyes were wide and blind to the world around her, but focused on something the others could not see. At times she let out yelps of pain or fright, throwing her arms over her head as though to ward off unseen forces that seemed to assail her from every side.

The Papago women told the curandera everything they had done. They had tried to give her strong tea and tried to put her in an herbal bath. They had burned candles all night, trying to drive the evil spirits away, all to no avail.

"There is a devil in her heart," said the curandera, "and he will not let her go."

Concha, wrapped in a blanket, seemed not to notice the curandera's presence. Still, when the old woman took her hand, Concha followed her peaceably. The curandera led her north for a while, back along the path of the river. There a crude shrine had been constructed out of adobe bricks containing an unrecognizable image. On every protruding ledge or level space, candles had been placed and allowed to burn down, so that the entire shrine seemed to be in the process of melting into the ground. It was there and not there, as though half in this world and half in the next.

"Here," said the curandera, stopping Concha before the shrine, "you must pray to the inocente buried here to take this devil away from you. This is a place where uncontrolled passions led to murder, where a man killed his own grown son for talking to the man's beautiful young wife, not recognizing him for his own. This innocent soul takes care of those who have been wronged, as he was."

Concha fell to the ground before El Tiradito, heedless of the stones beneath her knees. She appeared to pray for a long time, her lips moving soundlessly. As she did so, the curandera lit a single candle and placed it before the shrine.

"You must come and pray to El Tiradito once a month at

this time of the moon until you can no longer feel the presence of this devil," said the curandera.

As she helped Concha to her feet, the curandera looked into the young woman's eyes. They were dark and turbulent, as though a storm turned within each iris.

"But you must not ask for more blood," said the curandera, regarding her with concern. "Too much has been shed already. It can only bring pain in the future, if not to your future, then to somebody else's."

Concha did not answer her, pulling her head and face deep within the folds of her blanket. But she followed the woman back to the Papago village and seemed cognizant of her surroundings for the first time. Concha began to eat and help with the chores, and lost that look of a soul recovered from the brink of death. She told them where she had come from, but she did not tell them everything.

After two weeks, Mrs. Moreno could not stand it any longer. She missed Concha's quiet presence, and the children cried for her every day. She insisted that Concha was alive. So Mr. Moreno hung up his butcher's apron and got on his horse and rode down Meyer Street, asking people if they had seen Concha, until he came to the Indian part of town and was directed eventually to the adobe house where Concha was living.

Concha tried in her way to tell him what had happened. Mr. Moreno asked who had done it. When she told him, he could not believe that it was George Vaughan. He thought she was lying, and returned to town without her.

At home, Mr. Moreno told his wife, and the wife, who loved Concha and wanted her back to take care of her children, went to the widow Vaughan and told her what Concha had said. To everyone's surprise, George, who was hardly older than Concha, about eighteen, stepped forward and confessed. He said that he loved Concha and wanted to marry her. His mother was horrified. It was one thing to go with loose Mexican women, but to take an Indian woman by force offended her higher sensibilities. She put it down to his lack of a father during the formative years, George's inability to channel his baser appetites into hard work as his father had done.

Mr. Moreno rode back to the Indian settlement with the good news and told Concha that George wanted to marry her. To his surprise, she refused. Concha said that she never wanted to see George again in her life, or leave the Papago. Mr. Moreno returned to town with her answer.

George was very unhappy, but the widow Vaughan was even more so, for she was very religious and had a place to uphold in the church and the community, and her son had shamed them. The Morenos were unhappy as well, for they had been friends with the Vaughans, which was how George had first seen Concha. But Concha was the most unhappy of all, for she found that she could not bleed, because she was with child.

The Papago sent word to the Morenos on Concha's condition. This time, Mrs. Moreno would not be deterred. Mr. Moreno was again sent to the Indian settlement, which was by now getting used to seeing him. He told Concha that they would take care of her and her baby if she would only come back and live with them. She could mind her own baby along with their children, and she did not have to marry George Vaughan if she didn't want to. That is what Mrs. Moreno told him to say, and that is what he said.

This seemed to suit the Papagos, who by now had all appointed themselves her guardians. Concha did not wish to go back. She was afraid of George Vaughan. But the Papago were very poor, and here she was about to bring another mouth into the world to feed. She felt that she, a stranger from Sonora and no kin of theirs, had imposed on them enough.

So Concha went back to the house in town. The Morenos were true to their word, and took her back to help them, and raise their babies, and clean their house.

Mrs. Moreno watched Concha, quieter and more withdrawn than ever, now with dark circles under her eyes from sleepless nights. And sure enough, her waist began to thicken and Mrs. Moreno helped her let out her dresses from those of a girl to those of a mother-to-be.

That winter, just before Christmas, Concha gave birth. All through her confinement, dazed with grief, Concha had thought that she would hate the baby, would try to get rid of it if she could. But when she saw the baby girl and held her in her arms, something inside of her broke. She cried and cried and held the baby close. She was all that Concha had, this innocent, all of the family left to her.

To everyone's great and everlasting relief, the baby did not have red hair. Concha could not think of a name for her, knowing little of what were considered appropriate names for little girls in Tucson. In El Arbolito, she would have been named after a flower or an object of natural power or beauty. So when Mrs. Moreno suggested Rosa, Concha liked it right away. The Rose of Tucson.

For Rosa was like a little rose, with her dark eyes and brown hair, not black Indian hair, but dark hair with waves, and her delicate rosy skin, neither brown nor white. The whole family doted on the new baby, and the children had to be restrained from carrying her everywhere in their arms like a favorite doll.

Concha did as the curandera advised, visiting El Tiradito faithfully before each new moon and leaving a candle behind. She did this even after she returned to the Moreno household, rain or shine, even when she was too tired to see where she was going. She began to do the laundry in addition to her other chores in exchange for a little money, so that she could pay back the curandera who had saved her, as well as give a little something back to the Papago family who found her wandering in the street and took her in.

George Vaughan, always his mother's bane, became even more of a problem after that time. He began to drink heavily and frequent the part of town where whores and games of chance could be found at any hour of the day or night. There was talk that the widow Vaughan, fearing that her son would never marry and there would be no heir to the family business, might arrange to kidnap the baby girl. Or that George would do it himself. Concha was very fearful during this time, and the family tried to never leave her alone, even taking her and the baby to church with them, although Concha had never shown any previous interest in that institution.

After seven years, George Vaughan's body was found one Sunday morning in the barrio of El Tiburón, a knife thrust so deeply between the ribs that the tip of the blade was said to have broken off in the spine. He was thought to be the victim of a fight over cards. In a town used to violence, people talked about his death for months.

After hearing of George's death, Concha slept peacefully for the first time since all of this had begun, knowing that he could not hurt her again or steal her beautiful child.

What Concha could not know was that through her prayers to El Tiradito, she had cursed herself as well, for Mrs. Moreno's China pearls in their red silk bag grew heavier and heavier with moisture. Mrs. Moreno could hardly lift the bag that contained them. The pearls began to mourn for Concha and weep, for they knew what she did not, that Concha would never be fortunate in love.

Walking Home

Concha moved slowly down the street, favoring her left ankle. Her feet hurt, her back hurt, her bones seemed to grate together as she moved. She had three more houses to clean that day before returning home, long after dark, to a supper of posoles and tortillas that her daughter would have left for her. Rosa would be asleep, would rise early with her mother to help with the morning chores.

Somewhere people were celebrating. She could hear laughter, a guitar carelessly strummed. A woman's voice was saying "Aye, chico!" seductive and admonishing at the same time. Concha walked on through the dusty streets, lifting each foot carefully over the uneven bricks and stones. She deferred to the big men in their boots, pausing and turning sideways without effort to pass like water through the crowds. It had been a long time since she had had anything to celebrate.

Once, Rosa had brought home a tomato—big, ripe, juicy. She said a man gave it to her, an indio from the countryside. He said it was for her soulful eyes.

They had made a feast of the tomato, cutting it carefully in half in a zigzag pattern the way Concha's mother had taught her, adding salt and a tiny bit of cilantro to make it savory. Then they had eaten it, laughing, as though eating like kings and queens, so seldom did they get anything fresh. Concha went without food some days so that she could buy goat's milk for Rosa. Rosa's eyes were full of soul because her stomach was usually empty, and Concha worried about her only daughter, her only love in the world, her life.

If it were not for Rosa, she could not go on; she would have thrown herself in the river long ago, the saints be damned. But Rosa needed her, needed Concha to hold up her head and clean rich people's houses as she had always done, except for those few years when Dr. Martinez had loved her. Even with her baby, he had married her and she had been a respectable woman in a fine house, eating tomatoes whenever she liked.

Concha held up her head and walked.

And then she heard a voice behind her. It was under the rumbling of wagons, the creaking of carriages, under the shrill voice of a woman who thought she had been cheated, the coming and going of many people, shouting, laughing, dogs barking—but she heard it, nevertheless.

Concha stopped walking and slowly turned. The ground seemed to tilt beneath her feet. To hear that language, as a grown woman, after so many years, was like having someone speak to her in the language of her dreams, or call out her secret name, the name that she knew and kept only to herself.

"I know you! I know you!"

The voice cried out harshly, persistently, and as she peered back through the people and the dust raised by their passing, Concha finally made out a man close to the ground. He waved a powerful hand in the air, wrapped in a rag. As she looked, Concha could see he was seated on a board on wheels, and as she approached, tentatively, she saw that his stained pant legs were cut off short, that his legs ended above his knees, and the stumps were bound to the board with wide leather straps, as one would cinch a saddle to a horse.

He placed both hands on the ground, the knuckles cushioned by rags, and propelled himself towards her with a peculiar hopping motion, all torso, all muscle, a grotesque, shortened parody of a person. It was Beto.

Concha felt the tears start to her eyes, tears like birds upon her cheeks. How could she have more tears.

She fell upon her knees next to Beto and embraced her brother.

"Dios mío," she said, over and over. "Dios mío."

"Ya, ya," he said, patting her back. "Enough."

"What happened?" she asked. "What happened to you? I thought you were dead for years."

So there, her dignity forgotten, kneeling in the dust next to a filthy beggar for God and everyone to see, Beto told her his story.

"I was on a train," he said. "A compadre got me on a train going west. We heard there was plenty of work in California.

"But I had a spell, and you know when I'm like that I can't move, can't hold on, and so I fell off the train, under the wheels, and the wheels cut my legs off.

"By a miracle, there was a doctor nearby, visiting the town where I fell, and he saved my life. Otherwise I would have bled to death, especially if those pendejo railroad people could help it. The train didn't even stop.

"I don't remember any of it. I was in heaven with our father, talking to him. He told me I would live a hard 'life,' but I would survive. 'Keep moving,' he said. 'Don't let them catch you.'

"When I woke up, I was how you see me. But I've kept moving, as best as I know how," he said, indicating his legs, his platform.

"The doctor helped me and charged no money. He was young and not yet corrupt."

Concha wept and wept as he talked, birds on her face, rain on the ground. She wept for all their agonies, for all their travels and hardships, for the ranchería they would never see again, for their mother, for their father he had seen in heaven, for the others who had died or disappeared or gone mad.

And she cried for her old name that was lost, Shark's Tooth from the Sea, that had been taken from her so long ago. It was that which Beto had called out, that had cut like a knife through the noise and dust of the street, cut into her heart like a ripe tuna and made it bleed tears from her eyes.

Then she was done. Concha wiped her face and gathered her bags and parcels and stood up and brushed off her dress.

"You must come home with me," she said.

"You have a house?" asked Beto.

"Only a room," she said. "But it is a place to sleep, a safe place."

"Bueno," said Beto, and slung a sack across his back, all he owned in the world.

Down streets and across ditches they went, and where wheels could not roll, Beto picked himself up on his overdeveloped knuckles and propelled himself forward a foot at a time. His thighs strained at the leather straps that held his board to him, but the straps held, and Concha could see that he had traveled many miles, many places this way.

Coming to the house, Concha was hit by the fact that she lived up a narrow, steep flight of stairs.

She stopped abruptly.

"I live upstairs," she said. "We will have to carry you."

Even as she said this, she knew that even with Rosa's help, she could not lift Beto and maneuver his awkward shape up the stairs.

"It's all right," he said. He didn't seemed surprised or even disappointed. "I'll stay here. Just bring me a little something to eat."

Concha smiled gratefully, her smile that he remembered from their childhood, when he would follow after his big sister like a puppy. Concha hurried up the stairs. Rosa was startled to see her mother home early, so animated, her rebozo askew, her eyes wide with excitement.

"Come!" she said. "My brother is in the street! We must take him some dinner."

Grabbing the pot of beans and a shred of cold meat, Concha handed Rosa the tin plates shuffled together and wrapped in a shawl. They descended to the dirt street where Beto waited, smoking, against a far wall, a shadow within a shadow of the building.

That night they built a little cooking fire at the end of the lane, where it ended in a sandy arroyo. Beto shared their beans and meat and coffee while he told them of his travels, and praised Rosa for her beauty, and didn't ask where her father was, which Concha appreciated, because that was a story she had tired of, an old story that never would have an end. Only she would end, a piece of the story.

She learned that their mother and Javier Oposura had died at Casas Grandes. The soldiers had come there, too, and killed many people. Even in a holy place. Beto had been raised in Arizona by another family, and worked as a scout for the American army in their battles with the Apaches for some years before his accident.

Beto was proud to own no furniture. Things came between people and the truth. By remaining clean, pared down, a man who ate what was offered him and slept where he could, Beto's vision had remained clear. He was a man who could discern the true nature of things, whether they were good or evil, whether they meant something or nothing, whether or not they would have importance to someone in the future. Beto, by remaining free of things, could tell their true names.

Concha asked Beto if he thought la corúa was still alive.

Beto looked at her, his eyes slits in the firelight. "He got run over by the train," he said. "I saw him. He may still be alive in the villages farther south, but in Arizona and California, he is dead."

Who knew that there would be nights like this? The air tasting of her yearning for the old times, the old places, yet the proof before her that everything was gone, everything was as dust burned to ash in the fire?

Concha tried to hold on to what was left. She stroked Rosa's hair, pulling loose from its braids in the temperamental way it had, and thought of her own mother stroking her own hair when she was small. But this was hard. She could only remember Chiri brushing out the black, black hair of her little sisters, cooing and clucking over their beauty like a hen, so that she could do up their braids in white ribbon.

Concha realized then, watching her brother smoke in the dying firelight, that she had spent her life yearning for a past that didn't really exist, and never had. Her yearning was for what she had never had, a place nearer to her mother, a moment of recognition that never came.

Resting her hand on Rosa's shoulder, listening to her breathe, Concha realized that all she really had was the present, both good and bad. Rosa was getting older and was beautiful, and soon she would marry or go away with a man. Concha felt time moving around her like the river, flowing on, taking bits of her away, bringing by bits of her past.

Even as she thought this, Beto looked at her and said, "You better get that one to bed. It's late."

Concha rose, lifting Rosa to her feet, and guided the sleepy girl towards the steps to their little room.

"Good night," she murmured to Beto, who remained in his place. He seemed to have forgotten them already.

"Mmmm," he grunted. She knew that in his head it was already tomorrow, that he knew which train he would be on, that this day, like all the others, had been numbered and put away on the calendar in his head.

Concha saw that she would always remain part of his past, and their chance encounter was just that, chance. She knew then that nothing she could have done, could ever have done, would have changed things—either for herself, her sisters, or her brother. And if it did not make her feel better, neither did it make her feel worse. She just felt that she knew one more tiny thing. The river still flowed on.

The next day Beto was gone.

That evening the landlady, Mrs. Klein, said to her husband, "The neighbors saw Concha in the street last night, squatting like a common woman. With her daughter, too, sharing their supper with a crippled beggar."

Mr. Klein eyed his narrow wife over his evening paper. He drew on his pipe and blew a few puffs of smoke.

"That was right charitable of her," he said. "But see that it doesn't happen again. So's all the beggars in town don't think we're running a mission here."

Mrs. Klein was pleased with her husband, for she knew that he would have the right answer. She passed the word to Concha late that evening, who bowed her head and promised that it wouldn't happen again. Concha doubted that she would ever see her brother Beto in this life of sorrow again.

·II·

ROSA

How I Came to Be Different from My Mother

Growing up in the Morenos' house, I knew nothing but love. I did not want for food and I played with the Moreno children as though they were my own brothers and sisters. I did not get pretty new dresses like the other girls, Elsa and Julieta, but sometimes I got their old ones. Be grateful for what you have, said my mother. And I was.

I helped to feed the animals, the chickens and goats, and helped to cook or carry water or do whatever else was needed. In my village, my mother used to say, a girl always looked her best to carry water. That phrase, *in my village*, sometimes meant the beginning of a story. Or sometimes it just meant that there was work to do, and this was how she expected me to do it. When I did something in a way she did not approve of, she would say, "No es costumbre"—it is not the custom. But what is the custom in Tucson, I would ask, and she would look away and not answer. Then I felt badly and did as I was told.

My mother, Concha, did not like things to change. She was

afraid of many things. She was afraid that if too many things changed she would be left understanding nothing at all.

But the thing that she was most afraid of, especially when I was very small, was that my father would try to steal me. If a man with red hair ever tries to talk to you, she would say, a very white man with red hair, you must run away.

This was confusing to me, in part because I had many questions about this man, my father. One of the questions was, how could people have red hair? I had never seen anyone like that. Everyone I knew had black hair, and I had seen a few people with lighter hair, brown. Once a woman passed in a carriage and the other children pointed and said "Look, una güerra," but under her hat, I could see that the woman was just old, with whitish hair. I did not understand why the others made a fuss over someone who just looked old, although she was in a carriage, and I liked her hat.

But people did not have red hair.

"Like the blacksmith's building?" I asked.

"No," said my mother.

"Like a bird? A cardinal?"

"No," said my mother.

"Like a burning red coal?" I asked.

My mother stopped. She did not like these questions. Now her face turned inside, the way it did when she struggled to say something she did not know how to say or did not completely understand.

"Yes," she said finally. "It was like a burning red coal."

But the way she said it, I could not tell if she meant the color of my father's hair, or the way it felt when he hurt her.

That was the way she put it, When he hurt me. That's why I was born, because the man with red hair had come into the house when my mother was alone and hurt her. So she was afraid of him, and was afraid that he might try to steal me.

And so I had many questions, but as a little girl, I was happy.

One of my duties was to help Mrs. Moreno with her flowers. This was one of the things that my mother did not understand. She could not understand why people would carry water to grow plants that we could not eat. She understood flowering herbs, because they were medicine, and chilis and tomatoes and squash. She even understood corn, although it was hard to grow and took much water. But she thought flowers for the sake of something to look at were a waste of time and water.

"Flowers belong outside," she would say.

"But they are outside."

"No," she would say. "*Outside.*" And she would make a wider gesture, meaning the world, the land outside of the farms and corrals of the people around us, meaning the mountainsides and the desert, the land outside of Tucson. "Flowers belong to God."

But Mrs. Moreno loved her flowers, liked to cut big bunches of them and bring them in the house on Sundays. She liked to smell them and press them between heavy boards to keep in with her clothes. So I carried water for Mrs. Moreno's flowers and learned from her how they grew. They were almost like people, in that some flowers liked some things and some flowers liked others. They seemed to have personalities, and Mrs. Moreno even talked to her flowering plants as though they were children. She would carry them around in their pots, asking them if they wanted more shade or more sun, asking them if they needed to be pruned, or apologizing as she cut off an errant branch.

"This will just hurt for a minute," she would say, in exactly the same tone she used with her children. I would laugh, thinking she was just trying to be funny, but now I'm not so sure.

My mother thought I laughed too much, and told me to cover my teeth when I laughed.

"Es costumbre," she would say, then look at me in exasperation when I laughed again. "My mother used to laugh all the time," she said. "You are just like her."

But I knew that I was not. When Concha told me about her mother and her village and the hu'uki where her mother told stories, I knew that I would never be like Chiri. Chiri had been very brave, and although I was braver than my mother, I was not like Chiri at all.

As I grew older, I came to see that the heart of my mother's world was the hu'uki that belonged to her mother, Chiri, and her tía Pancha. Concha's world radiated out from it, like the framework of a basket. Everything she knew about it began with the stories she had learned in the moist semi-dark of the women's place. And every story she heard was connected to that place and told her how to live her life in that place.

As we prepared food for the Morenos' supper, my mother would tell me about the frijoles and trigo, the beans and wheat, that they grew in her village. A little corn was grown near the river, where it was easy to water. But they also harvested a great deal of food from the land and mountains around them—frutas del campo, as she called them. At certain seasons, they could gather pitihaya, uva lama, and the fruit of the saguaro. Coloraditos and chichiquelites grew at the edges of their milpas, where rocks or other natural interruptions in the land made it impossible to clear the fields for planting. Here the wildlife gathered and ate both the wild and cultivated foods, and provided game for the village.

She never used the old language in front of la Señora, but waited until we were alone. She did not want Mrs. Moreno to think that she was una india cruda.

But as my mother spoke about these things—the planting, gathering palm and weaving it in the hu'uki, the ceremonies and fiestas that marked the passing of the seasons in her village— she became a different person. My mother seemed to expand from the quiet, demure woman I knew into someone larger and darker. When the language of the old people peppered her speech, she spoke with a confidence I never heard in her Span- ish. Her face was different, and she moved her hands in a differ- ent way when she told the old stories about the old ways. These were the things that she knew about, was sure of, because they had been passed down for so many generations that it wasn't something she had been forced to learn later in life. They were a part of her in a way that life in Tucson would never be.

However, my mother claimed that the Opata had once lived near Tucson.

"We passed this way," she would say, indicating the area to the east of town as though it had happened just the other day. Although the Opata had moved south over several hundreds of years, they could, she said, stand on a high place and point northeast and see the place where they had come from, could tell stories tied to the places that still bore the names they had given them—Bacadéhuachi, Bavispe, Chiricahua, Chihuahua. The stone buildings their ancestors had built still marked the mountains and valleys, the stone walls they had built to make level ground and hold the precious water when it fell.

The Opata had built the mission at Tumacácori, she said, and helped the priests to bury their treasure before the mission was abandoned to the Apache. That was the way of the Opata, she said, to work. They mixed adobe and built churches and cities, and they farmed the good river soil. Once they had grown fine cotton—chinapa, she called it—and were famous all over the Indian world for it. They had never been warriors, she said, anxious to steal from their neighbors, but were not afraid to fight, even the women. When the Spanish had come, they agreed to help fight against the Apache, and for hundreds of years served in the Spanish and Mexican armies in all-Opata regiments. Her father's father had been a soldier, and she was very proud of this.

To the north and east of these places, the pueblo people still lived, maybe cousins. That was the known boundary of their world.

"We were good friends with all of these people," she would say. "The pueblo people used to come to Sonora once a year to trade, even when I was a little girl. Muy buena gente."

My mother's family had passed back this way when they went to Casas Grandes. Like a great movement of wind or weather, the people had swept north and east against the mountains, against the Apache, through the canyons and cuts and waterways where they saw the earthworks of the ancients. This is what my mother told me, that they crossed the mountains to the ancient pueblo of Casas Grandes and heard the words of the healer who came to visit for a while.

At each step of the way the old people had said, This was once ours. Our people lived here and built this, they farmed these barrancas and made these old stone buildings. They were a great people who came down from the North. This was once ours. And the Tarahumara looked at them from their lofty houses and the Apaches sat on their patient ponies and watched them pass, but did not attack. Even they saw that this was something holy.

And at each crossing, each place where valleys came together or roads merged, they came across more people swept up in the tide of faith. Some carried the very old or infirm. Others came as though fulfilling a manda, dragging a cross or walking on their knees. All spoke of El Tecolote as though they had waited for him all of their lives. He was the messenger, the owl whose voice meant death for the enemy.

My mother was part of this. She traveled with her mother. She carried her brother Beto much of the way while her mother helped her twin sisters, the sisters my mother, Concha, always felt that she had lost. They traveled with a man called Javier Oposura, Javier the fierce-hearted, who came to be with Chiri after her husband was taken away on the train by the Mexican soldiers.

After that she wouldn't talk anymore. The patterns of her conversations were always the same.

I came to realize that, in her terrible journey to Tucson, not only had my mother lost her family, but she also felt as though she had come to live on the edge of the known world, teetering on the edge of a precipice, and would never be comfortable living here.

The stories of this land were not her stories, the gods — Papago, Catholic, or Protestant — were not her gods. God only spoke to her through the ceremonies, the dances, the visit to Magdalena. God knew San Francisco and the river valley of her birth. She felt that he could not hear her cry so far from the land of her birth. He could not hear her cry over the screams of the train whistle, the din of so many people. He could not hear her whispered prayers over the clatter of china dishes in every kitchen. There were so many people here with so many things, and they were all from somewhere else.

I knew other people who had come from the towns of Sonora. They found places to live, learned to speak Spanish that others understood, bought houses and sold things to make money, and sent their children to school. They found a way to live in this place. But maybe they had not come alone. Maybe there had been enough of them, enough familia, to help each other, to comfort each other on the dark nights and hungry days when it seemed that they would not survive. By the time my mother got to Tucson, she was all alone.

I realized that my mother, who easily succumbed to susto, could never travel far. She would always be looking for Apaches or soldiers or redheaded men, would always look fearfully behind her in the dark. And no wonder.

Even if I ever got to New York to see the Indians with porcupine hair, the kind I had seen on a lamp in Alma Prieta's shop, I knew I could not take my mother with me. As long as she was apart from her village and her people, she would be a woman out of place. I knew that my fate would be alone or with someone else. Tucson was my home, but I understood that it might not always be my place.

Early on, I saw what the world had done to my mother and what could happen to me if I was not careful. So I covered my teeth when I laughed and stood up straight when I carried water. I was always polite and obedient and tried not to complain if things were not right. But I hid my mother's language as well and learned to take care of Mrs. Moreno's flowers. Even more, I learned to love them almost as much as she did, especially the roses that were my namesake.

And this was how I came to be different from my mother. I grew up at the forebearance of people who were not my family, having nothing that was really my own. Everything I wore, everything I ate, was borrowed. I understood that I might always be dependent on the charity accorded to the poor and fatherless.

These are things I thought I understood, but I was not sure I could change them. By the time I was fourteen years of age, when we were alone in the world, what I had to do was make sure that my mother and I had something to eat each day if I could help it. But I was ready to go out into the world and take care of myself, with God's protection, when the time was right.

✝

S u s t o

Elsa was the youngest of the Morenos' children and my best friend when we were growing up. She was lively and full of mischief and got me into more trouble than if I had been by myself. She often did things that my mother did not approve of, but since she was Mrs. Moreno's daughter and not her own, my mother did not scold Elsa as much as she scolded me.

We both loved music. We tried to learn every new song that we heard, repeating the words over and over to each other until we got them right. The house was not too far from Carrillo's Gardens, a beautiful place full of flowers, where famous musicians used to play. We used to go with the older girls and stand outside of Carrillo's Gardens on long summer evenings to hear the music and see the people in their fine clothes going into the fiestas that were held there. We did not have the money to go inside, but we could hear the music and the people laughing and having a good time.

Once a stern-looking man saw all of us children standing there in a bunch outside of the wall and we started to run away, thinking he would yell at us. Instead, he beckoned us inside, where he let us stand in a little courtyard and listen to the music for a while.

I will never forget that. Qué encantado. We could smell the beautiful fragrance of the roses. There was a fountain in the center of the courtyard, and just beyond it, we could see women all dressed up in expensive dresses of every color.

"Mírala!" Elsa kept exclaiming as she saw one, then another girl or woman dressed in her finery. There were Chinese lanterns hung on wires above the garden that cast a beautiful and mysterious glow on the people below.

A group of musicians dressed in fine suits were seated in chairs on a platform raised a little way above the surrounding area. They were not playing yet but tuning their instruments. Standing with them, talking to the band leader, was the most beautiful woman I had ever seen in my life. She wore a red dress covered in silver lace, and her hair was held in place with large silver combs. The hair around her face was in perfect waves that framed her dark eyes and pouty mouth.

"She's the singer," hissed Elsa, and we stared raptly at her. As she talked and moved, we could see that she wore silver shoes. She pointed at the music, and on her hands were gloves that left her fingers bare, held in pace by a loop around her middle finger, so that her arms and the backs of her hands were covered in silver lace.

In front of the orchestra was a dance floor, although no one was dancing at the time. The men and women stood or sat at small tables around the edge of the floor, talking and laughing as they waited for the music to begin. It was like paradise. The man who had let us in stood and watched us, obviously enjoying our youthful pleasure at the sight.

Suddenly the musicians raised their instruments. The violins scurried up the stair steps of the music, and the big basses joined them in the familiar, low *plunk-plunk* rhythm. A lone musician stood and played his silver trumpet, then the beautiful singer stepped forward. Just for a moment, I thought she looked at us, staring at her with our mouths open, and I thought I saw her smile in our direction before she squared her shoulders, took a deep breath, and began to sing.

Just as the orchestra begin to play, the man who had let us in scooted us out again into the night air. As he did so, he told a man who had joined him that he felt sorry for "las inditas." This made Elsa very mad, because she wasn't an indita but a Mexicana. I didn't care. I was just happy to be admitted, if only for a few moments, to the closest place, I thought, I would ever get to heaven on earth.

We ran all the way home, Elsa and Julieta and me, hoping that we had not been missed, for we had been sent to the store for something. But already my mother was standing anxiously in the doorway, looking up the street this way and that for us, and I was sorry to make her worry.

"Where have you *been?*" she asked.

Julieta held up the bag to show that we had been to the store, but it was empty, for we had forgotten all about it. We had to admit where we had been. My mother scolded us for walking around alone, but Mrs. Moreno just gave us a look she had, one I often saw her give her daughters that showed exasperation but not too much anger. The boys were treated differently, and "might as well be from a different tribe," as Julieta put it. They were given pocket money and allowed to come and go as they pleased.

Later I found out that it had been Señor Carrillo himself who had let us into the gardens, the owner and a great man in Tucson who owned a lot of properties. He was what Mr. Moreno called "a self-made man," the sort of man Mr. Moreno admired very much.

When we were about seven or eight, Elsa's older sister Julieta began to take singing lessons. She had a beautiful voice but could not follow a melody. A friend of the family's suggested that she should study music with a Professor Escobar, Professor of Instrumental and Vocal Music. He came to the house one afternoon to meet Julieta and see if she had any talent.

He was very portly and had spectacles that he tucked into a tight waistcoat when he was not using them. The Professor had her sing scales, up and down. We were watching from the outside, on the veranda that Mr. Moreno had recently added across the front of the house. He kept building on a little at a time as his family grew and as he had more money.

Julieta was singing scales and kept losing her way. I started adding a note at the end of each scale, the right note. At first the Professor thought it was Julieta and was very surprised, for I was in tune and Julieta was not. Then she pointed at us and said it was not her and he got very red in the face and chased us away. He did not like it that we had fooled him. We were giggling like mad by then.

But I saw that I could sing at least as well as Julieta, and I began to sing scales outside in the corral as the Professor had shown her. I remembered the singer from Carrillo's Gardens and wondered what it would be like to sing and dress up like that.

I told my mother that I wanted to be a famous singer when I grew up, to sing in front of an audience, and she frowned.

"In my village," she said, "only the cantoras sing in public. And only for special occasions at the church or in procession. They know many things that you cannot know before they begin. They train for many years with another cantora. Otherwise, women do not sing in public."

Nothing more was said about it, especially since I knew that we did not have money for voice training. I did not stop to think where I would get money for fancy dresses or anything else. But I still loved to hear the music at Carrillo's, and sometimes imagined myself dressed up like those ladies who sang with orchestras, and what a romantic life they must live.

I don't think Julieta's voice lessons lasted very long. I think that they were expensive for Mr. Moreno, but it was something that Mrs. Moreno and Julieta had wanted. She never forgave us for making fun of her that day. We did not mean anything by it. We were little.

This was about the time that we started going to school. At first, Mr. Moreno did not want Elsa to go. He thought that she was too young and should stay home with her mother. But Mrs. Moreno saw how much the older children were learning, and Elsa wanted to go, too. She could use her older sisters' books, Mrs. Moreno said. Chui got his own set of books, since he was a boy. So Mr. Moreno finally said that Elsa could go if I went with her, so that she would not have to walk alone. The younger children did not stay in school as long as the older, so she would have had to walk home alone.

So I got to go to school. This made my mother very nervous, and it is when she started to tell me again not to talk to any strangers or to go with any redheaded man if he tried to take me away. By now I thought that the redheaded man was like la llorona — not a real person as much as just someone the adults talked about to scare us into obeying them. But there were bad men, I knew. Sometimes men tried to talk to Elsa's older sisters and make them go with them. Mr. Moreno said it was because there were not enough good women in Tucson, so the men, especially the Americanos, were always looking at the Mexican girls. So Elsa and I walked to school with her older sisters, and home by ourselves for lunch. Then we stayed home and practiced our lessons or I helped my mother with her work.

It was not too long after that, maybe the spring of our first year of school, that I saw him. I didn't actually see his face, because there were a lot of people in the street, but as soon as I saw that hair I knew that it was him. He was tall and stuck up above the other people in the street, so I could just see a black hat and the hair that was as red as a burning red-hot coal.

I tried to run away, tried to tell Elsa that it was him, the red-headed man and that we had to run away, but I couldn't talk, I couldn't even move right. Instead, my arms and legs began to twitch in a way that I couldn't control. Elsa had not been paying attention and was a little bit ahead of me. When she saw that I was not with her, she turned around and said, "Rosa, what is wrong with you?"

That's the last that I remember, because then I remember falling. I was so scared. I was so sure that the redheaded man was going to catch me and take me away from my mother and that I would never see her again. I was falling and it was getting dark and my arms and legs would not obey me. Elsa was screaming at me. The tall skinny man with the red hair under his hat was getting closer, but that's all I can remember.

When I woke up, a crowd of people were standing around. I looked but I did not see the redheaded man. A family with a carriage stopped and took me home to my mother. They put me on the big bed in the Morenos' room. Mrs. Moreno gave them some money. My mother was crying, standing over me and praying and crying, but after a while my arms and legs grew better and I was able to sit up and drink something.

"Just like your mother," said Mrs. Moreno. "You suffer susto very easily." But she did not seem too mad.

I was afraid to tell my mother that I had seen him. I was afraid that she would not let me continue to go to school if I told her. She gave me strong tea that she grew in Mrs. Moreno's corral. She said it was for susto, and that her mother had given it to her when she was growing up. It was strong, but it did not taste bad. My mother did not ask me what caused the susto, so I did not tell her. I don't know if she ever found out.

But about a year or two after that, something happened to the redheaded man and I think he died or went away. No one ever told me exactly what happened. After that, my mother did not worry as much as before, and even seemed happier in some way, as though there was a duty or an obligation that she was done with. She probably felt safer, too, if she thought that George Vaughan was gone.

She took me once a few years later to see an old woman in another part of town. We walked and walked until we came to a big house that was set back from the street. It had a slanted roof and tall, narrow windows across the front. There was a spiky wrought-iron fence all along the street, and we had to let ourselves in a little gate and walk up to the front door. It was very spooky to me, but my mother had told me I had to be on my best behavior. I had borrowed a dress and shoes from Elsa to wear on this visit.

The woman was very large and sat in a big chair. She was all dressed in black and wore a long string of beads with a crucifix on it around her neck and hanging down the front of her dress. There was a little dog that stayed in a basket beside her. She asked me a few questions and looked at me very closely. Maybe she was trying to see if I looked like my father. She gave me a picture of herself and told me to keep it in case we did not see each other again. Then she kissed me on the cheek and held me close for a moment. She smelled like camphor and old clothes. It seemed very awkward and strange, as though she did not do this very often. I didn't know if my mother expected me to act happy, but I tried to smile.

I was glad to go home after that visit. On the way, my mother told me that the woman was my father's mother, who was a widow and was all alone now. That meant that she was my grandmother, although she did not feel like family to me. Again, I had so many questions that I did not know where to begin, or if my mother would even answer them. How could she be my grandmother? She was not at all like any of the grandmothers I knew, who were happy old women who liked to give sweets to their grandchildren. She did not live in a house like other grandmothers. Even though she kissed me, she did not seem exactly happy to meet me. The kiss still tingled on my cheek, as though I had been branded.

It made me wonder what it meant to be related to someone, to be part this or part that. I was part Irish, because of my father, and I was part Indian, because of my mother. But I felt more Mexican than either of them, like the Morenos. I even looked more like the Morenos. We all spoke Spanish and lived in the same part of town and went to school together with the other Mexicans. Sometimes the children called me india because of my mother, but not very much, because some of the Mexican children were much darker than I was, and were probably just as india as I was, if not more.

I don't remember that I ever saw my Irish grandmother again. She was very old, so she probably died soon after that. But I kept her picture. It had been taken in a studio. She was seated very straight in a chair and looked younger than when I met her. But she was wearing the same crucifix around her neck and had the same stern expression on her face—the look of a religious woman who was used to getting what she wanted.

In some ways, I am glad that my mother did not take me to see her more than that one time. She might have come to expect more of me than I could have given her. To act like the daughter, or granddaughter, that she never had.

After that first spell in the street, I continued to have spells of shaking and the inability to move my arms or legs. My mother's teas did not help me. Sometimes Elsa and I had to stay home from school because I felt very weak for a day or so after these nervous fits.

After an especially bad fit, Mrs. Moreno sent for a medical doctor to come and examine me. His name was Dr. Martinez. He came to the house and looked in my mouth and my ears and asked many questions. He looked in my eyes and made me follow his fingers with them. He pressed all over my head in a strange way with his thumbs to determine its physiognomy, as he called it, and asked if I had taken any bad falls in which I had hit my head.

My mother, standing by my side, answered these questions with downcast eyes. I could tell that they made her uncomfortable, this stranger asking personal, physical questions. Women took care of women in her pueblo, and she had been brought up to be very modest and distant with men.

"And the señorita's father? Does he have these fits?"

I giggled that he called me a señorita, as though I were rich, but my mother was silent for a moment.

"Her father is dead," she said. I looked at her because it was the first I had heard that. My mother was stone-faced, like a statue.

Dr. Martinez did not pursue that line of questions. He removed his stethoscope and placed it in his black medical bag, which gaped beside the bed where I sat for the examination in my nightgown.

"I am not absolutely sure, but there is the strong possibility that your daughter suffers from el baile de San Vichy, for which there is a cure. I recommend cold baths each morning for ten minutes at a time."

My mother nodded her head, hardly seeming to hear him. She was probably still disturbed by the mention of my father. I think now that she would have liked to pretend that I was sent to her by angels without the involvement of a man.

Dr. Martinez softened his formal manners slightly. "Get dressed, my dear, and I will talk to your mother out in the parlor."

Elsa came in and asked all about the medical examination as I put my clothes back on. My head tingled where he had pressed it.

After that, my mother bathed me faithfully every morning in cold water, even if it was cold outside. She did this in the kitchen area, which doubled as a bath house, since water could be heated outside. But not for me. I dreaded getting up in the morning to face my cold bath, but my mother insisted. She seemed to believe in Dr. Martinez's cure, and talked about how she had always bathed in the cold river with the other girls. All the men of the village were supposed to stay away on those days, and they used to sing and play in the water, cupping their hands and hitting the surface like a drum. I tried to do this in the narrow tin bathtub, but I could not.

About this time I also began to have strange and very vivid dreams. I asked my mother what they meant.

"You must only tell your dreams to someone who knows how to interpret them for you," she said. "That is a very special gift. My little brother Beto had it."

She had told me about her brother Beto, who, even when he was little, was visited by people from very far away to have him tell them about times and places that no one else could remember. I asked if Dr. Martinez could tell me about my dreams.

"No," she said, "do not tell him, or he will think that we are ignorant Indians."

It shocked me to hear her talk that way about ourselves, because she had never said anything like that before, even when the other children said things to me about being la indita. But my mother understood something about the world that I did not yet understand—that there were two worlds, the Indian and the Mexican, and that people treated you differently depending on which world they thought you were a part of. Indians were drunk and lazy and superstitious, while Mexicans were hard-working and tried to get along with the American vecinos, even when we did not understand what they were doing. The dreams seemed to belong to the old world, the Indian world, and would have to stay there in order for Dr. Martinez to do his work.

Dr. Martinez came back once every two weeks to see if I was getting better. The Morenos paid for the first visit. He did not charge for his services after that. All the children in the barrio loved him. Dr. Martinez would stop in the street and lift his arms and allow them to search his coat. He carried little candies in his copious pockets, and the triumphant children would hold up the trophies they found there before popping them in their mouths.

We were always happy to see him, for he filled the house with laughing and joking. It made me feel important that he came to see me, and I stopped being so ashamed of my fits. After that first visit, he always saw me in the parlor like a regular visitor, with my mother present. As they talked, sometimes I felt that they did not even remember that I was there. My mother grew to trust Dr. Martinez and even told him a little bit about herself, about the village where she had been born. Dr. Martinez was also from Sonora and had come up from Altar with his parents when he was younger, so that he could go to school.

In spite of the discomfort of the cold baths, the spells began to lessen in frequency and severity, and eventually disappeared altogether. My mother insisted that I continue to take the cold baths, especially if I seemed especially nervous or weak.

About this time, Dr. Martinez asked my mother to marry him, and she agreed. This surprised me very much, because I had always thought of us as a permanent part of the Moreno household. My mother told me that we would live in our own house in another part of town and have plenty to eat, and she would not have to work so hard. My mother was twenty-six at that time, and had worked very hard since she was a girl.

Mrs. Moreno cried. She had gotten my mother back once, from when she had gone to live with the Papago, but this time my mother was leaving for a happy occasion. Elsa cried because I was her best friend and we had done everything together since we were little. They were sorry to see us go, but we promised to visit often. My mother felt bad at leaving Mrs. Moreno with all that work to do, so she found a woman who could come and do the washing and cooking and cleaning that my mother had been doing all these years.

Mr. Moreno's carnicería had done well, and he had continued to add onto and improve the house as time had passed. We had lived in our own room at the back of the house for some time, a room with its own doorway opening onto the corral. Even so, once my mother had cleaned up after the last meal of the day, she liked to sit outside in the ramada and work on the mending until it was too dark to see. Although she would not admit it, I think that she grew to enjoy the flowers in Mrs. Moreno's garden and the many birds that were attracted to it. It was a place where she had come to feel at home.

Mrs. Moreno insisted on having a wedding portrait taken of my mother and her new husband. We all went to the studio across the way and watched as they stood and stood while the photographer got them right. My mother did not like this. I'm not sure that she approved of having her photograph taken at all, but she could not refuse this one last request from Mrs. Moreno, who, after all, had been good to us all this time.

Nogales

After my mother married Dr. Martinez, we went to live with
him. But Dr. Martinez felt that there was more opportunity for
him in Nogales, so we moved there. I had never been out of
Tucson before. Nogales was a very small place to live. There was
not a regular school there, so I was no longer able to attend.

Dr. Martinez set up his practice in the front rooms of a
house and we lived in the back. My mother assisted him. She
was busy from morning until night washing linens and steriliz-
ing his medical instruments. She had to measure out the pills
that he prescribed to people, and take care of me and the house
as well. By now I was older and able to help a lot, but I did not
see that my mother was working less than she had when we
lived with the Morenos. Dr. Martinez told her to do things as
though she was his servant more than that she was his wife,
and I'm sure many of the patients did not know they were married. He often went out alone to visit his patients and did not
come back for a long time. But my mother did not complain,
and was grateful to have her own home. She used to walk

around picking up or touching each object as though it was magic.

Since we were now a little farther south, my mother spoke of going on a pilgrimage to Magdalena, a holy place where her people used to visit. She wanted to thank San Francisco for her good fortune by visiting on his feast day, October 4. She wanted to take him an ofrenda, make him something special. But she did not seem to know exactly what, and she was too busy helping Dr. Martinez to think about it. My mother thought she might see some of her own people as well. She spoke as though I would go with her, but whether or not Dr. Martinez would let us go was never discussed.

When my mother was not pregnant after one year, Dr. Martinez began to give her medical examinations as well. He very much wanted to have his own children, not just me. He could not understand why my mother did not get pregnant. He made her eat special food, rich food, and drink milk, which my mother did not like. She got fatter, but she did not get pregnant.

At first Dr. Martinez was very kind. In the evening, he would tell my mother that she worked too hard, and make her sit down and put her feet up. But by the next morning he seemed to have forgotten all about it, and spoke to her sharply if she did not bring him something right away when he asked for it. She had to help him with the difficult cases, the men who had been thrown from horses and had broken bones, or who had been hurt in fights. These men had to be held down while their bones were set and their wounds cleaned out, otherwise they would die.

After two years my mother was still not pregnant, and Dr. Martinez began to change. He accused her of not wanting to have any more children, of using secret Indian potions to keep from getting pregnant. My mother would weep and deny this, for she really did want to please Dr. Martinez and have more children. After assisting him all day in the surgery, my mother made a meal for us, and often Dr. Martinez was perfectly silent throughout. Sometimes he looked at me strangely, as though resenting the fact that I was my mother's child. I pretended not to notice and kept as quiet as possible. I missed the Moreno children, especially Elsa, and would not have minded having younger brothers and sisters. I was old enough to take care of them while my mother assisted Dr. Martinez.

My mother wanted more than anything to provide a good home for me, to live what she imagined was a normal life in Nogales or wherever he wanted to go. I could hear his voice late at night, talking querulously to my mother, and I knew that she sat and wept quietly.

Dr. Martinez began to stay away from the house more and more, especially at night, and then the worst thing happened. I heard him come home late one night and speak loudly to my mother. I got up from my bed and stood by the door to listen. My mother was crying more loudly, crying as though her heart would break, and saying, "Please don't do this to us. I will do whatever you want, whatever you say. We can even raise the child here, but don't leave us alone."

I could not understand what she was talking about, but when I got up in the morning Dr. Martinez was not there. My mother sat dry-eyed in the front parlor, wearing the nurse's apron that she wore when she attended him, but there were no patients there.

"He has gone," she said, seeing me.

I went to my mother and put my head in her lap, for I could see that she was scared, and so I was, too.

"He has gone to live with another woman who is carrying his child," she said.

And then I cried, for I did not know what would happen to us.

My mother and I moved to another house that Dr. Martinez found for us, for he wanted to keep his medical practice where it was. He moved back in with his new wife. At first he paid the rent for us, but after a few months, the landlord came and said that the doctor had not paid the rent and we would have to pay it or move.

My mother was very sad during this time. She sat all day looking out the window at the people and horses passing in the street. She almost didn't seem surprised when the landlord said that the rent hadn't been paid. My mother sighed and got up and put on her rebozo.

"I am going to go out and see if I can find some work," she said. "Stay here. I will be home later today." She was gone for a long time.

It turned out that my mother went to the houses of the people who had come to see Dr. Martinez. She knew which ones had some money and which ones did not, so she went to the people with big houses and offered to clean or cook or do laundry for them.

Even so, we had to move to a little room at the back of another house, a room smaller than the one we had lived in at the Morenos', up some steep outside steps on the side of a hill. We had no furniture, only a bench that ran along one wall and served as both bed and table. We cooked outside over a small fire on a grill that held the pan up above the flames. My mother said that even in Mexico her family had a stove built onto the side of the house. After all this time of Dr. Martinez making sure that we ate well so that I would get over my fits and my mother would have children, all he left us with were beans.

And this is how my mother spent the last years of her life, cleaning the houses of people she had once assisted as Dr. Martinez's wife. Sometimes I went with her to scrub floors while she did other work, and the people pretended not to know us, as though by treating us as strangers they could spare us the humiliation of my mother's abandonment. We sold some of our nicer clothes that we did not need anymore. Even though some were things that had once belonged to Elsa and no longer fit me, it was hard for me to do.

My mother never spoke badly of Dr. Martinez. I think that she felt that it really was her fault for not being able to have more children, and it was what she deserved. I asked once why we did not return to Tucson, for I missed my former life, I missed school, and I especially missed Elsa.

She shook her head. "Too much has changed," she said. "Besides, they have Luz now, and so they don't need us."

Luz was her friend who had gone to work for the Morenos. If we returned, the Morenos would have to let Luz go. It was the first time I realized that we had really just been servants and not like family. It was the first time I realized how important it was to have familia to take care of you during hard times like this. My mother had lost her family in Mexico, and so we had to clean other people's houses to earn a little bit for food and rent and to keep body and soul together. I had never worked so hard in my life, but I was older now, and stronger. I no longer had fits or weakness in my arms and legs except when I was just tired, and I kept my dreams to myself.

✝

Beto

I had just loaded up a basket to take to the arroyo to wash our clothes when my mother burst into our little house.

"Leave that," she said.

I was startled to see my mother home so early, looking so animated, her rebozo fallen back from her face, eyes wide with excitement.

"What happened?" I asked. "What's wrong?"

"Nothing is wrong. I found my brother. My younger brother Beto, who I thought was lost. He is outside. We must take him some dinner."

I did not understand why he could not come inside to eat, but did as I was told. We took the pot of beans that was always ready and a little meat that had been given to us. We wrapped up our plates and went outside to where my tío Beto waited. At first I could not really see him, for it was still bright outside and he was in a shadow against a building, a shadow within a shadow, smoking.

At first I was horrified, sure that my mother had made a

mistake, that this beggar could surely not be her own brother, but some man who had convinced her of it. His clothes and his skin were dirty, but he did not keep his eyes downcast like a man of no honor. He smiled at me like a real uncle, as though he had just met me in the front parlor of a house.

"Don't worry," he said to me. "I'm not as scary as I look."

I felt myself blush that he had read my feelings.

My mother bustled us down to where the arroyo began at the end of the dirt lane with more energy than I had seen in her since we left Dr. Martinez's house. There we collected sticks and built a little fire in the sand. We shredded the piece of meat and mixed it in with the beans and put them on the fire. My tío Beto moved himself with just his hands, lifting himself and pushing himself forward a few inches at a time through the rough soil. Then he planted himself firmly and resumed his smoking. As the food heated, he started to talk about all of the places he had seen riding the railroads, wherever they took him. My mother seemed to relax, to unfold as he spoke, all of us sitting in the sand as if we had supper there every day.

I tried not to stare at this man, my tío Beto. He barely seemed human to me at first, more like a stone statue left over from some ancient, fallen city, his legs broken off and his arms as big as clubs. But as I watched him talk and move his hands, I saw more and more of my mother in him—the way he turned his head, the proud line of his mouth, the way he bit words off from the air when he grew excited about something.

And I wondered at the difference that had came over my mother for those few hours, how comfortable she seemed wrapped in her shawl and sitting on the ground. I finally lay my head in her lap as they talked and nestled into the warm sand as the air cooled, the crackling fire made of sticks a familiar noise. I had not done this for a long time. I could not understand why I was so sleepy.

My mother and tío Beto talked about a place that had existed long ago, before the soldiers and the Yaquis began to fight, before their own people had been forced to walk north for their lives. They talked about a time even before the Chiricahua had ranged across the desert on their fierce ponies, when the Opata, their own people, had lived peacefully along the river valleys and grown cotton. They reminisced about a ranchería in Mexico where they had been born, a place they remembered as beautiful and peaceful and full of food.

I struggled to stay awake, to listen as strange fluting words gradually crept more and more into their speech, trying to make out what it was that my uncle called my mother, for it was a word, a name, I had not heard before, until I slept, imagining the calls of owls, or the wind blowing through mesquite trees to make buzzing and clicking sounds.

This was a world that I did not know, and though I wondered if we should be watchful — outside at night where bad men like the redheaded man or who knows who else might find and steal me as my mother had always warned — I was not afraid. Instead, I wondered what it would be like to listen to these words every night, to be wrapped in a blanket of kin and kinship and family, as my mother and uncle must once have been. The words entered my sleep and bloomed like cactus flowers in my dreams. The talk was like a canopy over my head, a ramada woven of words, that lulled and protected me from the foreign world I would always have to call home.

The next day my tío Beto was gone.

Later that night, when my mother returned from work, I saw the landlady, Mrs. Klein, talking to my mother. She did not like what she had seen. My mother bowed her head and apologized for us, for camping in the arroyo like common people. She promised it would never happen again.

My mother was different after that night. I think she was deeply embarrassed in front of Mrs. Klein, about keeping me out in the street at night with someone who looked like my uncle did, and was afraid we would lose our room. She spoke no more about her brother, and less about her village in Sonora.

"Where did he go?" I asked.

She motioned into the sky, the air.

"Para allá," she said. Out there. Out into a world that was always changing, that promised nothing, yet sustained her brother like a spider on the wind.

As October approached, I could see the old hunger in her eyes, but she did not talk about making the pilgrimage to Magdalena anymore. I did not know what to think. Maybe Mrs. Klein scared her about her Indian ways. Maybe her brother scared her. He did not scare me. At least not after a while.

My mother worked harder than ever trying to make money, but her health did not improve, and finally a morning came when she could no longer rise from her bed. I went to work without her that day, cleaning the houses that she cleaned, working from first light to dusk. I did not go to school in Nogales anyway, since only the wealthy families hired teachers for their children. Dr. Martinez had not been interested in sending me to a teacher, and now that my mother and I were alone, there was no money anyway.

My mother was concerned about me walking into the houses of strangers by myself, but we had little choice at that time. If we were to eat, then I had to work. We had not heard from Dr. Martinez for a long time.

The Lamp Shop of
Alma Prieta

My mother never got over her sadness of marrying Dr. Martinez and having him leave her. We never passed by our old house when we went to other houses or to buy food, and I think that my mother deliberately avoided that street. She did not want to run into the woman who now lived with him and was giving him children. My mother grew weaker and weaker, and sometimes she could barely get up in the morning to start the fire. She missed her husband and could think of nothing else, night and day. She could not sleep or eat. My mother, who had been beautiful and full of life, withered away before my eyes into an old woman.

More and more often I had to go in her place to work, so it was just as well that I was not in school because I would have had to stop anyway. Besides, we could not have afforded to buy books. In Tucson, I had shared Elsa's books. I tried not to think about what Elsa was doing while I scrubbed floors or hauled ollas full of water to heat for laundry, but sometimes I couldn't help it.

A girl in one of the houses was nice to me. Her name was

Olga and she was a little older than I was. She liked books, too, and sometimes lent me some of hers to read.

Olga could read and write and do sums. Her father bought her the books and excused her from some of her domestic duties so that she could study. They saved their kerosene so that she could read at night, and she often read the textbooks to her family, even the arithmetic. They were very proud of her. Soon she was offered a job in a store and was able to bring home money to her family. It was the first time any of them had made money "without making mud on her skin," as her father said.

One day Olga asked me to go to a meeting with her. She had heard a man talking in the street about religion, about leading a good life, and he had stopped her and given her a paper with an address on it showing where a meeting would be held.

It was a group that was against drinking, and she thought that was a good thing. On Sunday mornings in Nogales we had to step over the bodies of men who had come into town the night before and gotten drunk. Or worse, some of these men went home and beat their wives and children.

After I finished cleaning for the day, I hurried home to ask my mother and she said that it was all right if I went with Olga. I changed my working dress for my better one and went to Olga's house to accompany her to the meeting. It was held in the front of a house that had EL TEMPLO DE DIOS lettered on the outside. It did not look like a church either outside or inside. There was not a single crucifix to be found, only a few benches arranged so that we could be seated while different people talked and prayed and sang. Both men and women stood up to do so, something I had never seen when I had gone with Elsa to church in Tucson. They talked about how much God loved us, as a father loved his children or a shepherd his sheep and would go out on even the darkest night to find a lost lamb, and it made me think about how I had never really had a father.

The people were very kind and seemed to be buena gente. They served food after the service. They gave us pamphlets to take with us and read, and I took one, if only to have something to read.

I returned to the meetings with Olga whenever I could after that because I especially liked the young minister. His name was Gabriel, and he had not lived in Nogales for very long, either. He, too, had no family, for they had told him not to come back after he left the Catholic Church. He, too, did not have a father, for his own had left home long ago when he had gotten into trouble with the authorities. After a few months, he asked to marry me. I told him he would have to obtain permission from my mother.

Gabriel came to the house and was kind to my mother. In spite of his upbringing, he seemed comfortable coming into the homes of poor people. He said that we were all equal in the eyes of God, rich and poor alike, and that it was even easier for a poor person to go to heaven. I had never heard anyone talk like this, for Mr. Moreno had been very interested in having his business be successful, and had greatly admired the men in Tucson who did well. Also, Mrs. Moreno liked to have pretty things for both herself and her children, and I knew that she could not unless Mr. Moreno made money at his carnicería.

Gabriel asked where my mother had come from in Mexico, and told how his father had traveled all over, prospecting for gold and living with the people. He had gone to live at Casas Grandes, and a great many people came to hear him tell stories about God.

Yes, my mother had said. She said that she had once heard of such a man. I thought she had told me that she was there, that she herself had seen El Tecolote, but she did not say this to Gabriel. Much of my mother's life was like this, first one way, then another. Maybe the truth lay in between or nowhere at all.

Sometimes I thought that things that might be true in one world, the old one she grew up in, might not be true in this one, the one I had to live in, and somehow she understood that.

"But did you see him?" I asked later. "You always said you went to Casas Grandes. But when Gabriel was here tonight, you said only that you had heard of him."

My mother stood over the fire. She did not look at me.

"What I did not tell you is this," she said. "What I did not tell you is that when we came to a crossroads, my mother turned to me and said, now you go with El Gusano. He was a man who used to come to our village to trade things.

"She took my brother Beto from my back, where I carried him, and got on the horse with Javier Oposura. She left me standing there with my two sisters and El Gusano, the man nobody wanted to have looking at her, and said, you go with him now, he will take care of you."

My mother stood gripping an olla with both hands. I thought she would crush it between her hands.

"She sent us away with that man, in another direction from Casas Grandes, north instead of east."

More time passed and my mother did not move.

"A little while after that, they left me and went on."

"They left you? Where?"

"Just . . . on the trail. The wagon broke and they had only the one horse. Some other man took my sisters and left."

I did not understand. "Why?"

"Because I was not pretty like my sisters." Then my mother's shoulders moved a little and she turned to me. I could see tears on her face.

"Lucky, eh? That's when I came to Tucson. I did not know how to get home, or what would be left for me. So I came north."

I did not know what to say. What her mother had done sounded like a horrible thing. But I could not say anything against my own grandmother, whom my mother had loved so much.

My mother wanted to be sure about Gabriel. She did not trust people as easily as she might have once.

Does he truly love me? she asked. I didn't know.

"At least I know he does not want me for my money," I answered, laughing. But my mother did not laugh. It was after that when she decided to take me to see Alma Prieta.

It always scared me a little to go near the dark shop at the center of town. It was flanked on either side by perfectly ordinary storefronts, but the lamp shop of Alma Prieta, oddly enough, seemed rather dark. Even at one P.M., when the sun was so high and hot that everyone was preparing for siesta, and the dogs were circling for the best spot in the shade, the shop seemed to pull a cloak of darkness around its shoulders.

Not that the shop was open then. Alma Prieta's kerosene lamp and novelty shop was only open in the evening, late into the night, when people had time for such things. Such things as they came to her shop for, that is.

In its front window was a lit kerosene lamp glowing through a wide rawhide shade and illuminating a scene that never failed to draw me closer as I passed by. On it was painted a series of scenes of Indians and white pioneers. But I had never seen such Indians, either here or in Tucson. They must, I decided, live in New York. New York was a place I had heard of, a place full of fabulous tall buildings and people who spoke and dressed strangely. It is a place where it snowed and there was a port with huge ships that floated on the water like smokehouses. People got on those smokehouses and sailed across hundreds of miles of water to an even stranger place called Paris.

New York must have been where the lampshade was painted and where those Indians lived. They had their heads shaved except for a small piece like a porcupine, and rode tall horses and lived in pointed houses with poles sticking out of the top.

The other side of the lampshade showed Anglos bundled up in many clothes in horse-drawn wagons. Even the wagons were covered up, as though wearing huge bonnets. In each scene, a few men rode ahead of the others on their horses. They appeared to be leading the way. But since all of them were heading in the same direction on the shade—to the left—the two parties would never encounter each other.

It was the perfect solution to the West—the bravos leading the way, followed by the children, the women, and the dogs, then a little space followed by the men pioneers, followed by their families. As long as they continued to circle the lamp-shade, they would never run out of frontier. They would never run into each other and have to fight.

I never saw Alma Prieta fill the lamp or even turn the shade, yet it seemed to burn perpetually, and I knew its every detail by heart. I was sure that on even the darkest, latest nights, the kerosene lamp continued to cast its spell in the heart of Nogales, seen only by drunks and men returning from courting their sweethearts.

I had only seen Alma Prieta from the safety of the doorway, speaking to a visitor, the corner of a folded handkerchief pressed to her lips. But I had heard a great deal about her. Because Alma Prieta was born with a harelip, she was supposed to be able to speak with the spirits of the dead.

I did not know why this was true, but everyone in Nogales believed it. In fact, Alma probably did more business with the spirits than she did in lighting. There was always someone who had an urgent question for those who had gone before.

I was fourteen years old and about to marry when my mother took me to see Alma Prieta.

She took me, she said, to make sure that I should marry

this preacher who was sure to take me far from home, probably far from the desert my mother had always called home. He was from a town in a different part of Mexico, Saltillo, and himself an exile cast off by his family.

"What kind of a future is that?" my mother asked. "What will you give your children? Two exiles, no money, no land."

So she took me to see Alma Prieta one night. It was at ten o'clock, about the time that her serious customers were beginning to trickle in—women with sick children, unfaithful lovers, men who hoped to see material wealth in their futures. At the back of the shop was a glass case full of strange and wondrous things: oils for warding off evil spirits or assuring good health, soaps for attracting a lover, powders and ointments for whatever ails, lottery cards, pictures of saints, and rosary beads made from the sacred beans and seeds of the desert—two powers in one. It was behind this case that Alma Prieta stood and ministered to her flock—the needy, adult children of the night.

Concha had spoken often of her own mother, Chiri. Most of the time she spoke of Chiri as though she were dead. But at other times she talked about Chiri going off to the mountains with an Apache-fighter, Javier Oposura. While I knew much about my mother's village, much of it was of the same nature—maybe this was true, or maybe that. Perhaps one was the way my mother wanted it to be, and the other was the way she feared it really was. In any case, I was pretty sure that my grandfather, Chiri's husband, had been taken away with the Yaquis and was probably dead. I was not as sure about Chiri, but here we were consulting with Alma Prieta to talk to my grandmother, so maybe she was dead, too.

There were many Yaquis in Nogales, including Alma Prieta. They stayed together and spoke their own language. They celebrated many fiestas, and on special saints' days or at Easter, the

Indian part of town was practically empty because the Yaquis had returned to their villages in Mexico. Some of the Opata returned home to their villages farther south, too, but things were more uncertain in the north country.

The night we visited Alma Prieta, my mother pushed me in front of her. She knew that I did not want to be there, and I was sure that Gabriel would not have approved. We made our way past the kerosene lamps and tins of fuel to where Alma Prieta stood, partly obscured by her supplicants. She stood with her head bowed, eyes closed, one hand pressed to her brow as though praying. In her right hand Alma Prieta held a silver hair clasp across which she rubbed her thumb, and occasionally she brought it to her nose as though smelling it. I understood without being told that she was about to speak with the spirits. We stopped short at the outer edge of the circle and waited quietly.

Suddenly, Alma Prieta threw her head back, turned her face to the ceiling, and opened her eyes wide. She seemed to be staring at something none of us could see, and began moving her hands in front of her as though talking to someone.

Alma Prieta lifted the hair clasp, then cast it away from her on the counter as though it had burned her hand. It rolled with a sharp rattle. An elderly man stepped forward to take the clasp before it rolled onto the floor, a look of consternation on his face. He folded it in a piece of cloth and kissed it. With wide, unseeing eyes, Alma Prieta turned towards the group of people and pointed with her now-empty hand towards us. I could see the harelip clearly for the first time, the separate parts of it exposing crooked teeth. With gasps and low mutterings, the crowd parted to form an open path between Alma Prieta and us, my mother and me, and my mother pushed me forward. I did not understand what was going on.

Alma Prieta grabbed my hand so hard it hurt, her eyes still wide and yet unseeing, and pulled me violently towards her.

She reached into the folds of her skirt and pulled out a lottery card of the Falling Woman, and held it out for all to see. My mother shrieked and fell to the floor. Susto, I thought, and tried to get away and go to her, but Alma Prieta held me fast.

Then Alma Prieta began to speak. A torrent of words. A gush of images, some sacred, some profane, many of which I did not understand. Clutching my hand and raising it towards the ceiling as she spoke, Alma Prieta's voice rose and fell like an evangelist's, speaking sometimes in Spanish, sometimes in Yaqui, and sometimes even in English.

I was so scared as I stood there, watching my mother lying on the floor. She moaned and rolled back and forth, her arms clasped around herself, as Alma Prieta spoke. I was afraid that I would have a fit myself, although I had not for almost two years.

Suddenly the stream of words stopped. Alma Prieta dropped my hand and seemed to sag beside me. She now seemed a small woman. Alma stood heaving for a moment, her temples wet with exertion. Then she tapped me lightly on the shoulder. Just once.

"Dios te bendiga," she said, and whatever had kept me rooted to the spot now released me. I went towards my mother, every eye upon me, people drawing back as I passed. I lifted my mother from the floor as she blinked and looked around her, seeming to return from a faraway place. Then she took my hand and stepped forward to throw money on the counter, more than I dreamed she even had, and we walked out onto the cool and quiet streets.

We did not speak a word as we made our way home, past the iron and wood gates now bolted shut against the elements of the night. Concha kept her head bowed, her body wracked by the cough that more and more took away her strength. We walked back through the quiet streets to the dusty lane where we lived, and Concha made a small fire to heat water for tea.

I fell asleep almost immediately, for I had worked all of that day before we went to see Alma Prieta, but I think that my mother stayed up late, thinking.

Concha must have heard what she needed to hear, for she said no more against the marriage. In the short time left when we were both on this earth, she never mentioned the visit to the lamp shop again.

After that, my mother bought a length of tulle and began to sew in the evenings outside as long as there was light. I thought that perhaps she was making a wedding dress for me, but she would not discuss it.

"It's a secret," she said, so I asked no more about it.

And so, shortly after my fifteenth birthday, Gabriel and I were married by another minister at El Templo de Dios. Olga was my best maid.

My mother died shortly afterwards. I think that she willed herself to live just long enough to see that I was not left alone in the world. She only asked one thing of me, that she be buried in a pure white cotton shroud as she would have been back in her beloved valley in Mexico. What I had hoped would be my wedding dress turned out to be just such a shroud, sewn with her last ounce of strength. She had known that she was dying all along.

They told me that she died of tuberculosis, a disease of the lungs, but I know that she died of a broken heart. She never recovered from the way that Dr. Martinez had treated her, or, I guess, from George Vaughan. My mother, Concha Canelos Martinez, was not yet thirty years old when she died.

†

Gabriel

When we married, I went away from my mother's house with the same case I had brought to live in Dr. Martinez's house when he was my father. Only now I was no longer a little girl but a grown woman and a wife. Olga told me that I must wear a pretty nightgown on my first night with my husband. But when we knelt by the bed and Gabriel asked the Lord to bless our marriage and make it fruitful, I knew that I had embarked on a new life as a child of God. Whatever he willed for us in the future would be our fate. I was no longer at the mercy of other people, but a handmaid of God.

As Gabriel's wife, I immediately assumed duties with the church where he was the minister. I was put in charge of the Sunday school, where ten to fifteen children of all ages and backgrounds were left in my care. At first I knew little more than they did, but with constant prayer and guidance from my husband, whose zeal for the Lord burned brightly, I learned a little more each day.

We made several trips into the Papaguería during this time,

where Gabriel exhorted against strong drink and meaningless ritual. Although each community had its chapel, Gabriel refused to preach there, as his break with his Catholic upbringing was complete and final. I did not see that God would be present in one place but not another, but I did not question this. My husband did not distinguish between Catholic worship of the saints and Indian ways, but considered them all pagan. His divide from his family was so violent that I, who had no family, wondered what they had done to make him feel this way.

Gabriel was greatly interested in reaching out to the indigenes and asked my help in translation. But what I knew from my mother were the words for food and children, not church and philosophy, and he quickly realized that we had spoken a language from the interior that was meaningless to the Papago.

For a while Gabriel met regularly with an old Yaqui in Nogales to learn his language and was able to understand enough to translate some passages from the Bible. He shared his labors with an American scientist traveling through the area who asked to borrow his notes. We learned much later that the man published the work, never mentioning my husband's name or offering compensation. Gabriel would have hoped, he said, to receive some money that could be used to print his Bible tracts, or at least pay the Yaqui who had informed him.

We spent the first summer of our marriage in Guaymas, a beautiful city by the ocean. I don't think my mother ever saw the water, but spent her whole life in the interior. I thought of my tío Beto, riding the trains, and wondered if he ever came here.

Gabriel was charged with supervising the construction of a new church in Guaymas, as the congregation had outgrown the little house where it met. With the help of a Chinese man, Gabriel was able to secure building materials at the best prices. At one point there was no money and construction ceased, but I did not mind spending a little longer on the coast. We could walk by the sea for free. Gabriel grew very sick at the end of the summer and then it was time to return to Nogales.

Soon after I was expecting a child and anticipated the first of our family with a mixture of fear and joy. The women of the church showed me how to cut and hem diapers and to Gabriel's great satisfaction, I spent my free evenings sewing clothes for our new arrival.

The night of our baby's birth was very long. I was in labor for many hours, too many to count, and although the midwife encouraged me to push as hard as I could, I could not get the baby to come out. I missed my mother that night more than any other time since her passing, sure that she would have known what to do. Our baby was born at five in the morning, small and weak after her strenuous fight. We slept most of that Sunday while Gabriel, with hardly a bit of sleep, preached that morning.

We named her Ruth, for she had followed us into a strange land as I was about to follow my husband. Whither thou goest, I will go. Whither thou lodgest, I will lodge. Thy people shall be my people, thy God, my God. Our precious baby lived only three months before returning to the Lord, too fragile for this world. She returned to live with the angels, Gabriel told me. While I believed him, I wept and wept at having her taken from me.

But more children came to us, and most of them lived. As my husband was moved from one church to another, as a community in need asked for him or God called him, we moved from town to town — Guaymas; Pitiquito; Las Cruces, New Mexico; a long time in San Antonio. We owned nothing that could not be put on a train or sent by carriage. I could cook anything in one big pot, stirring with one hand and holding a baby on the other hip. When I sat down to nurse, I had a little time to read and so continued my poor education, although I would never catch up with my husband. He studied Greek and Hebrew in the evenings so that he could read the originals of the Word of God.

Gabriel loved each of his own children very much. He named each after someone in the Bible—Ester, Phoebe, Daniel, Pablo who was converted on the road to Damascus. He spoke often of the twelve tribes of Israel and how ten were lost. At times I think he was trying to create our own tribe. In a way we were our own tribe, our own community, for as often as we moved, the family was the only constant in our lives. Because we were without families of our own, each child was a precious gift to Gabriel and me.

For an orphan, this was all I could ask for. My family has been my treasure on this earth. Wherever they go, they take a part of me with them. I have never gotten to New York, which is probably a different place from that which I imagined as a little girl in Tucson, but maybe one of my children will see it for me.

Alma Prieta had said something about my children and my children's children that strange night so long ago, that they would see and do things of which I would never dream.

But something else she said disturbed my mother—something about the blood of revenge falling on innocent heads. We have suffered, but He has also protected us from the worst, gracias a Dios. I do not know what Alma Prieta meant. If my mother, Concha, understood, she never told me. And unlike Gabriel's father, she never wrote anything down. That and many other things died with her. She is resting in Heaven with the angels, and my babies.

By the time we stopped on the way to Pitiquito to visit my tía Lucy Canelos, there were four living children. I had not known about my aunt until just before my mother died, when she told me of her sister. I do not know why. My mother had many

KATHLEEN ALCALÁ

secrets. When we inquired in town after my tía, we were directed to a little house on the desert apart from the other houses. My aunt welcomed us with open arms as though she had waited all these years for us and gave my husband some papers that would change him forever.

For the first time in all these years, Gabriel talked more about his father, who had been known to my mother's people as El Tecolote. He told me of his father's lust for gold and how it had led him away from the family. It was after many adventures that he went to Casas Grandes. After that terrible time when many were killed, including my grandmother Chiri, his father had fled north and not been heard from again.

This was a different story than I had grown up with, and it made El Tecolote seem more human. My mother's people had seen him as a powerful curandero who came to retell their stories, to affirm their place in the world. Until I met Gabriel, I had thought my mother was at Casas Grandes, but she had come by herself to Tucson instead, looking for her sisters. Had she gone to Casas Grandes, she, too, might have died.

Now my tía Lucy Canelos had these papers gathered from the floor of the desert, and Gabriel recognized his father's hand. They told the rest of his father's story, of his increasing devotion to things spiritual and his strong sense that there is a way to make the world a better place. This latter point appealed greatly to my husband, who had devoted his life to exactly that. These things also made Gabriel see his father in a new light, and perhaps forgive him a little for leaving the family so long ago.

120

·III·

shelly

The Girl in the Closet

If I just stay here, I will be fine. Before I shut the door, I got a box of crackers from the kitchen, so I will be fine.

It is dark and cool in here. It is quiet, quieter than in the main room of my studio apartment, where I can hear the traffic from the freeway. I like it in here. It is cool and dark and quiet. The phone rings, but I do not answer it. It stops, begins again, then stops. Now it is quiet again.

I just wish that I did not have to go to work tomorrow. I wish that I did not owe money for my college loan, and that I had enough to pay my rent for a few months.

But if I don't go to work, I will lose my job. And if I lose my job, I will not get a good recommendation to find another job. If I do not have a job, I don't know what I will do. There is no one to support me. My mother is remarried and has other children to take care of, and my father is drunk in front of a TV in a trailer in Brawley. My mother's new husband does not like me. He is afraid he will have to support me, too, so I cannot say how I really feel about my job when I visit. He sits there with those wary eyes, sort of jealous that I have a good education, a good job, while he works construction. He drinks, too, but not like my dad.

I tried to tell my mother about my boss once, but all she said was, "Well, what do you expect? Unmarried and living alone?"

"This is the United States," I said. "It's okay for women to work and live alone."

"Well, men will be men," she said. "Just do your job."

I even told her that a man had seen my boss yelling at me on the street one day, trying to get me into his car, and came up and said he was a lawyer and I could sue for being treated like that.

"Oh, honey, that would cost money," she said. "Besides, wouldn't you have to get up in front of a roomful of strangers and say what he did? It would be too awful, too embarrassing, for all of us. It would be shameful."

I had to admit that I agreed.

The best thing about being in the closet is that I am sure no one else is in here with me. No one can touch me, no one can hurt me. I am alone.

At least I can sit in here all night and feel safe. Maybe I will go out and get a blanket, which would be softer than the floor. But not just yet. Maybe after it is darker. I forgot to close the curtain, and he might be out there, might see me and know that I am home. Last week he came over and pounded on my door and yelled so that the neighbors could hear. I am afraid he will get me evicted from this apartment that was so hard to find.

Everything is so hard. Working. Driving. Keeping the car from falling apart. Looking nice for people while I feel that I am dying inside. Keeping my true feelings to myself so that I will not go on a rampage and burn down the building with him inside it. I see him tied up and lying on his office floor so that he is as helpless as I feel, that look in his eyes of being completely at someone else's mercy. So he will know how it feels.

How could I have taken this job? How could I have known what he would be like, since his assistant, Robert, interviewed me? Why didn't Robert say, Don't take this job, because my boss will eat you alive? Maybe he wanted company in his misery. Maybe he thought I was strong, stronger than him. Sometimes people think I am stronger than I am. I have gotten by by looking tough, by bluffing.

But this time I can't take it. Everyone helps him, no one helps me. They knew what it would be like for me, and no one told me. You are not the first, they should have said. We have seen lots of girls come and go, and they could not take it. I cannot take it, either, but I have no place to go. Those girls had families that loved them. Those girls got other jobs. Those girls knew the ropes, the tricks, the ways of the world, knew how to use what they had and get what they wanted. I am just me, and I have always gotten by working hard and being brave. But here no one cares.

The box of crackers is empty, and I am tired. Maybe it is time to go out and get a blanket. If I can stay below the window ledge, I should be able to crawl out and get a blanket and get back to the closet without him knowing I am home. If he is watching. If he is sitting out there in the dark in his car and watching.

The next day as I passed through the front hall on my way to work, the landlady sidled out of her office with that look that signaled she had something to say.

"Your boyfriend was here yesterday," she said.

I said nothing, but I waited.

"He was looking for you. Wanted to know if I'd seen you recently."

Still I said nothing.

"I said I hadn't, but I don't see everything." She waited.

I waited.

"He said he had some things to drop off for you, and wanted your key."

I froze. "I don't have a boyfriend," I said, "so I hope you didn't give it to him."

"I didn't," said the landlady. "I told him he should wait for you."

I could tell she thought she had done me a big favor, and expected to be thanked.

"Thank you," I said. "Please don't give my key to anyone."

"No problem," she said.

I hurried out to my car, my heart sinking. Another day. Why do these people call him my boyfriend? I wondered. Does he tell them he is my boyfriend? He must.

He's not my boyfriend, I wanted to say. What is he? My boss, my torturer.

Your torturer was here yesterday, they should say. *He wanted the key to your apartment.* Or, *That stalker called. He's so nice. He asked me to have lunch with him.*

Good, I would say. *You do that. Take his mind off of me.* I wished that I had told him I had a boyfriend when I started working there. A Hells Angel who was very jealous. But I didn't see, then, why I needed to lie.

Then I understood why people at work acted that way. I was the sacrifice. If he was bothering me, the reasoning went, then he wasn't bothering them. Simple. Sacrifice another young virgin on the rock of this man's ego. Who cares about me? I'll be gone in a few months, but they have to put up with him for years, until retirement. He's a senior vice-president and editor-in-chief of International Publications. He's the president's friend. The executives have lunch together, socialize at each other's houses. I, by contrast, have the company status of a squashed bug. I am one in a long line of assistants who has paraded through that office. They objectify me because he does. If they get involved, they can only lose. No one helps a loser.

I pulled into the parking lot and tried to steady my hands. I had forgotten to eat breakfast.

I picked up some of the company's new books that were on display in the lobby and promised the receptionist that I would return them. Among them was a book of photographs of Guatemalan women. The photographs were by someone I had met before, Karen Foster. We were working on a new book with her. Karen had come into our office and met with my boss, who was her editor. She was fortyish and dashing, wearing slacks and a white shirt with a scarf around her neck that made her look formal without looking as though she cared what she looked like at all. The photos were accompanied by essays written by a famous feminist and defender of human rights in Latin America. There were also interviews of the women written by Karen. All of the women were so eloquent that I felt she had probably taken considerable freedoms with whatever the interpreter had told her. Or the interpreter herself was a pretty good writer.

The women in Karen's book were captured in time. If young, forever young. If old, forever old and not dead. The turn of their headdresses, the embroidery on their huipils, the way their children were slung on their hips or their backs, all looked noble, perfect. The pots that they shaped with their square hands, the food that they cooked, everything looked staged, protected from what must be the reality of their lives. I stared and stared, unable to bridge the distance between what the photos said and what my own common sense told me.

The photographs made me want to be photographed so that I could look noble and beautiful and so that, by transference, my life could become noble and beautiful as well. In the meantime, I was stuck with humiliated and degraded, and Karen was overdue in responding to editorial suggestions on the text for her new book and would not return my calls.

Inside the photographs, everything was in focus, everything framed just so, only enough detail to enhance the central image—unchanging, enduring, beautiful. Outside was the dirt, the filth, the abuse, the hunger, rising before dawn each day to work unceasingly until it was too dark to see. Twenty or more years of continuous pregnancies, births, miscarriages, and deaths of infants, followed by a short old age. Soldiers coming in randomly to steal or torture or burn huts and crops.

I knew that many indigenous people felt that a photograph stole the soul of its subject, but I felt as though my soul was leaking away, day by day, under the relentless gaze of my tormentor. I longed to be safe within the clean, white borders of a perfect photograph. A mere afternoon before the lens of a camera seemed a much less painful way to lose one's soul than having it whittled away one insult at a time.

I went to the coffee room and filled a mug. I usually didn't drink coffee, unless I accidently forgot and took a sip, but warmed my hands on it so that I would be able to type. When I returned, he was calling my name. He told me to come into his office and take some notes while he talked. He loved to tell visitors that I was a graduate of a good college with a degree in journalism, then have me take a memo. I did as I was told, pretending to be invisible. Still, I could feel him staring at my breasts as he rambled.

Finally he asked, "Where were you last night?"

"When?"

"Late. I tried to call you."

"Oh, I was probably there. Sometimes I unplug the phone when I go to bed."

"What if there's an emergency?"

"No one needs me that badly," I said, standing up. "Is that all for now?"

"Yeah," he said, staring at me. "That's all. For now."

I picked up the telephone receiver when he walked out of his office later so that he would not speak to me. I let my hair swing low over my eyes so as to avoid eye contact, but still, I felt like a bug under glass with him watching every movement to see if I would break under pressure. Every dress I wore, every hand gesture, every piece of jewelry was weighed and measured in light of his ego. If I smiled, I must be open to suggestions, familiarity, intimacy. If I did not smile, I was in a bad mood, on my period, a lesbian.

I know that he shares his remarkable insights into my personality with his male colleagues—I can see it in their eyes when they pass me in the hall. Once, two of the men discussed what I looked like while I was standing right there, as if I was inanimate. I tried to break into the conversation, but they were apparently deaf as well. All the men here couldn't be this bad, could they? Or maybe it's just because I am the only Chicana and the others just don't care what happens to me. There was an accountant, a man, who had to be, but he did not acknowledge my existence, so I could not ask him.

I began randomly pulling papers out of files and throwing them away. This kept me busy the rest of the morning. At noon, I went out and splurged on a meatball sandwich. I had just made half the payments on my student loan, three hundred dollars at a time. It was a small victory, and I had no one to share it with but myself. Congratulations.

I celebrated by taking a long walk in the hot sunshine. Just to be around people who did not know who I was was a relief, a cessation of pain. A kind smile from a shopkeeper was the greatest solace available to me. I felt that if there had been any more animosity directed towards me, I would have shriveled up like a brown leaf under a magnifying glass in the sun. I tried not to think, just put one foot in front of the other until it was time to return. I knew he would not be in when I got back and would not return to the office that day.

When I got back, Robert told me he was getting married. His girlfriend, a lawyer, was pregnant. He was not inviting me to the wedding, which would be at the home of someone we both knew.

"You understand, though," he said. "I have to invite him. After all, he's my boss. And I can't have you both there. Besides, he's my buddy. He loaned me money."

I tried not to cry. It's not that I was dying to go to the wedding, it's just that it was one more thing. One more hurt, one more hand in the face pushing me away. Why wasn't my heart numb by then? Why did it have to keep feeling?

I went to bed early that night and tried to get some sleep. When I did sleep, I usually didn't dream. It was just blank darkness, followed by the terrible reality of waking.

But sometimes I dreamed. I dreamed that I was hitting someone as hard as I could. Sometimes it was my mother, sometimes my father, sometimes my boss. It felt really good to hit this person, to feel my fist connecting with flesh, grinding against bone. At the same time, I was screaming insults. It was horrible, and I woke afraid to sleep again. It was my true feelings, yet not the way I wanted to be. I felt as though their brutality had rubbed off on me.

Sometimes, though, once in a while, I dreamed about a man I did not know. I don't know if I had seen him someplace, or if I had just made him up out of my head.

He had green eyes and a gentle smile. Sometimes he was sitting across from me in a coffee shop, not trying to touch me or hurt me, just happy to talk. Surely I couldn't have met someone like this, so maybe my brain gave him to me as a gift, to make up for the horrible hitting dreams.

This man had sandy hair and green eyes and tended to wear khaki-colored clothing. There was an air of distraction about him, as though he had misplaced his keys while recalling something pleasant. His manners were mild and courteous, and women treated him like a younger brother. How did I know this? I don't know. He didn't seem to mind that I was Mexican, and didn't get that lascivious look that some men get when they find out, like every Mexican woman has a Tijuana whore inside of her just waiting to get out.

Every time I tried to look at him directly in my dreams, he seemed to fade from view. So I looked at my hands or out the window at the passing cars. Even though we were always in the middle of a conversation, I did not know what we were talking about, or anything about this man other than what I could see. I hoped that he was smart and had a sense of humor. I hoped that he was a college professor. No. College professors made me nervous. Maybe a scientist, a geologist. I wished him success.

Sometimes I hoped that he was Latino but not Mexican. Maybe something exotic like Argentinian. Something that no one could disapprove of one way or the other, but might make him understand me better.

I hoped that he was someone who would never know what a terrible person I was, what terrible thoughts I had, because I was afraid he would not come back to my dreams if he found out. A man who didn't exist, a dream lover, because no real lover worth spit would have had me.

I daydreamed about this man at work. I wrote him a poem. It felt good to have one safe image I could settle on, one person who wasn't likely to turn on me when I was not looking. I knew that I didn't want any real people close to me, to even touch me, and assumed that the existence of this dream lover was further evidence that I was losing my mind.

Ellen, an associate editor in People of the Americas, came bustling into the office the next day as though she hadn't been laid up for the past four weeks eating rice through a straw. She was the third person I knew of in the company who had developed Crohn's disease—a wonderful disease that eats holes in the lining of your intestine. And Crohn's isn't contagious—you have to earn it through stress and overwork. Or have a predisposition to it. Or, most likely, have a predisposition to working yourself to death.

"Ellen!" I said. "How are you feeling?" She looked thin and grey in her red business suit.

"Oh, fine, fine," she said, dismissive.

She stopped in front of my desk. "Are you busy these days?"

"Not especially," I said. "Why?"

"I have a project we may need your help on. You speak Spanish, don't you?"

"Yes, I guess so. I've never studied formally or anything, but I understand it."

"Good. We have a book on Native Americans under way, and we may have located some very interesting photos in a private collection in Tucson. The owner speaks primarily Spanish, even though she has lived in Arizona all of her life."

"I don't think that's unusual," I said.

"Well, anyway, we need someone to go there and work with her, find out if these photos are what Reuben thinks they are, remnants of an extinct tribe from the Sonoran Desert. Is he in?" asked Ellen, pointing at my boss's closed door. "Is he busy?"

"He's in there," I said. I watched the phone line blink on, then off as he hung up.

"Why don't you go ahead?" I said.

Ellen knocked, then opened his door. He greeted her with a hearty obscenity, and she closed the door behind her.

The possibility of escape was almost too good to contemplate. At this point I would have been happy to break rocks in a prison camp, just to be away from him. I had been thinking about prison a lot.

I couldn't hear what they were saying.

Robert came in just then, carrying an armload of papers.

"You aren't too busy with Karen Foster's book, are you?" I asked him.

"Are you kidding?" he said, dumping the papers on his desk. "I'm just making work to stretch it out. Everyone seems to be avoiding working with us these days."

I didn't say anything.

"Why?"

"Ellen says they may want to use me on a project in Arizona. They need someone who speaks Spanish."

"Sounds great, but who knows what he'll say. He may not want to admit he can do without you."

"He could hire a temp. Isn't your friend downstairs about to finish her project?"

"Oh yeah. Marci. She would be perfect."

"And he would like her, too."

"Yeah," said Robert with a smirk. "He would."

I could hear him fussing inside. Soon the two of them burst out.

"Look here," he said to Robert, ignoring me. "Ellen's department wants to use Shelly to research some pictures, but I told her we're really busy right now."

"Will they pay Shelly out of their budget?" asked Robert, looking at Ellen.

"Absolutely."

"Then we can hire a temp. Like Marci."

"Who's Marci?" he asked.

"You know, the woman who's temping in the Golden Years department. My friend from Georgetown. The tall blonde . . ."

"Oh yeah . . ."

"When would the project start?" I asked.

"As soon as possible," said Ellen. "The owner of the collection is in her eighties."

"Find out when Marci will be available," he said to Robert. "If she can move up here, then maybe Shelly can go—if we don't get too busy in the meantime."

I looked at Ellen and tried to give her a neutral smile. "I'll call you as soon as we know," I said.

"Great," she said.

He went back in his office and shut the door, emerging a minute later with his cigarettes. "I'm going out for a minute," he said without looking at me.

Reuben Alexander had edited at least a dozen books on the Indians of North America—the big, glossy kind. People bought them for their kids or for their parents who moved to condominiums in Arizona and wore a lot of turquoise jewelry. I assumed that they made a lot of money for the press.

I waited nervously outside of his office, wondering if he was going to quiz me on my Spanish.

The door to his office opened, releasing laughter, and Ellen came out to get me.

"So," he said, trying to size me up without actually looking at me. "Tell me about yourself."

"Well, I grew up in Fontana. I went to UC Irvine and studied journalism. My parents are from Mexico, so I speak some Spanish."

"You have relatives in Arizona?"

"No, I think they are mostly here in California. Some in Mexico. But I think my grandmother may have been born in Arizona. I'll have to ask."

"Do you have experience interviewing people?" Reuben asked.

"Just for newspaper articles in college. This is my first real job, and I've been here for a little over a year."

Reuben paused for a minute, considering. "We have a woman in Arizona who may have some very interesting information. Her family has been there for generations, and they have a lot of photos. Some of them may be just what we are looking for. Or they could be nothing at all. You think you can work with this old lady?"

"Probably," I said. "I have a lot of elderly relatives. They appreciate good manners."

"That's exactly right," said Reuben, sitting up. "Older people want to be treated respectfully. Her name is Josefina Mendoza. Family has lived in Tucson forever. A house full of stuff—some of it, I'm sure, very valuable. Her sons have a construction company, so they are fairly well off. The Arizona Historical Society tipped us off to her, said she might have some material that would interest us. I'm not sure how the family made the connection to the Opata. Maybe they were employed as construction workers or ranch hands. But the Historical Society says it looks like the real thing, and there's a lot that hasn't made it into any public collections. It would be great to include in this book."

"What's the book?" I asked.

"We're calling it *The Other Indians of North America and Mexico*."

"Isn't Mexico in North America?"

"Yes, but . . ." Reuben looked exasperated. "Nobody seems to understand that."

Reuben glanced at the clock. It was almost noon. "I think you will do just fine," he said. "Ellen will help you make the arrangements. You'll need to find a place to stay while you're there. I'm sure we will have some other stuff for you to check out as well."

Reuben stood and extended his hand over his desk. I took it and we shook before I left. He looked genuinely pleased. I was flying now.

I paid my rent in advance and prepared to leave. I called my mother and told her I was going. She seemed hurried and nervous. "John is working late tonight," she said, "and doesn't like me to tie up the phone in case he tries to call."

"When does he like you to tie up the phone?" I joked, but she did not seem to think that was funny. I didn't have time to ask her about any relatives in Arizona.

The night before I was supposed to leave, the phone rang, late. It was my boss.

"I'll miss you," he said.

"It's only for a couple of weeks," I said carefully.

"I hope you don't have any ideas about transferring. . . ."

I didn't say anything.

"Because I'll give a truthful assessment of your work skills."

I couldn't resist. "Meaning what?"

"That you are not a reliable worker. That you have a short attention span and can't be trusted with long-term projects."

I felt the blood rising to my face. "I'm the only person in your department who has ever stayed long enough to see a book from beginning to end."

"That's for me to judge. And for me to give the recommendations. So just keep that in mind while you are off on this little holiday."

I hung up the phone carefully, hoping that he wouldn't hear

the click and would keep talking to himself. Then I took the phone off the hook and double-checked that my door was locked before I finished packing. I was definitely going to apply for a new job at World Educational Resources when I got back. Maybe Reuben and Ellen would give me a good recommendation for my work on this book. Maybe the position in The Golden Years was still open.

Tucson

Mrs. Mendoza's house was located in a beautiful, older part of town. Some of the houses were falling down, but there were big trees and children playing in the yards. I pulled the rental car up to the curb and got out. The sun beat down on me and I wondered if Mrs. Mendoza would give me anything to drink.

I didn't need to worry. Leaning on a cane, Mrs. Mendoza answered the door herself. She was accompanied by a yapping dog. Mrs. Mendoza was a little confused at first about who I was. She struggled to talk to me in English until I said something in my slow, careful Spanish, which helped a little. I showed her a copy of one of Reuben's books I had brought along just in case and repeated the name of the publishing house, that I was here to look at her photos for a book. Finally she understood, and welcomed me inside.

The house was built in the old style, with a front passageway through which I could see a large and beautiful courtyard. Mrs. Mendoza led me into a sitting room decorated in plush red furniture. Paintings in heavy gilt frames hung on the walls, and small, breakable objects covered every flat surface. I've been in this room before, I thought, if not in this house.

Mrs. Mendoza insisted that I be seated on an overstuffed couch while she brought me something to drink. I helped her clear a spot on the low table in front of the couch and talked to the little dog that stood growling at me. I could tell Mrs. Mendoza really liked this, and was soon regaling me with stories about her dog, her grandchildren, and her garden. The dog, having done its duty, settled on a little pillow on the floor.

When about a half hour had passed, I asked if Mrs. Mendoza wanted to talk about the photos she had shown to Deedee, an assistant curator at the Arizona State Museum.

"Oh, those old things," she said. "Deedee was looking for pictures by a particular photographer, someone who was here for a while and took many famous photographs all over the Southwest. A man who dressed as a woman or a woman who dressed as a man, some such nonsense."

Then Mrs. Mendoza told me a long story about how her parents had dressed her older sister as a boy when they took a long trip into Mexico. This was before Mrs. Mendoza was born. It was a story about wagons and many place names and intimations of what might happen to young girls who were kidnapped or who otherwise fell into the wrong hands. Nothing direct, of course, but her eyes flashed behind her thick glasses whenever she implied the scandalous possibilities.

I grew drowsy under the web of words that seemed to coat everything in the room. I allowed my eyes to wander across the paintings on the walls, interrupting to ask if that painting was of Mrs. Mendoza's sister or if that was her mother whenever the appropriate character came up in the course of the story. In this way I felt that I could at least get a grasp of the characters involved, in case it came in handy should actual photographs ever be produced.

Finally my eyes fell on a large box in the corner. I could see something like a photo sticking out over one edge of the partially open box.

"Are these some of your photos?" I asked, emboldened by boredom.

"Oh yes. Yes! Of course! You must think that I am a foolish old woman, going on and on about the past. But let me see here!"

Mrs. Mendoza took the box from me shakily, and I took it back just long enough for Mrs. Mendoza to be seated in a chair before placing it in her lap. I found myself kneeling on the floor like a child.

"Are all of them in this box?" I asked as Mrs. Mendoza set the lid on the floor and began to lift first one, then another of the photos. They seemed all mixed up—late sixties, early fifties, and earlier, judging from the clothing styles and whether or not they were in color.

"Oh no, hay más. Muchos más!" Mrs. Mendoza waved her hand as though implying rooms full of photos elsewhere in the house.

Finally she seemed to find what she wanted.

"Here!" she said, adjusting her glasses. "Here is one of them!"

I tried to see what Mrs. Mendoza was holding, but she kept moving it back and forth in front of her eyes, trying to focus. This woman needed new glasses, I thought. She reminded me of my grandmother in her last years, barely able to sign a check at the grocery store.

The photo was a posed portrait of a woman in a white blouse and a long black skirt. She also wore glasses, and stood before a white column holding a book, one foot slightly in front of the other. She looked scholarly.

"This is . . . what?" I asked. I didn't want to plant ideas in Mrs. Mendoza's head if she could remember anything about the photos.

"This is a photo by that photographer. I can't remember her name. The girl's name. I'll have to ask my son. He would remember."

"Does he live here?" I asked.

"Oh, yes. Alberto. He visits me every day after work. I will remember to ask him when he comes today."

Mrs. Mendoza sat back from the effort, and I could see that she was tired.

"Maybe I should come back tomorrow," I said. "I could come a little later in the afternoon, and maybe you could ask your son about the photographer."

"Oh, no, no, I'm fine," Mrs. Mendoza said, but I could see that she wasn't.

"Well, I'm a little tired," I said. "I just got in today, but I was anxious to meet you."

"Oh!" said Mrs. Mendoza. "Well in that case, you should get settled first."

"Yes," I said, getting to my feet. The dog stirred. "Maybe I could come back . . . around four tomorrow?"

"Oh, no, I have errands to run with my son. Is two too early?"

"No, that would be fine."

I let myself out. It was unclear whether Mrs. Mendoza's son would be there then or not, but maybe she would remember to ask about the photographer.

The apartment was a furnished studio near the University of Arizona. It had that weird, yet comforting air of things that many people have handled but nobody cares about. I rummaged through the kitchen drawers for a can opener, thinking about the stark contrast between the apartment and the house where I had just spent the afternoon.

Mrs. Moreno's house, with its doilies, porcelain figures,

pillows and rugs, pottery and family photos, seemed stuffed with more memories than any single person could remember. It was a collection of mementos, of the particulars that are supposed to document a family, if not define it. The apartment, on the other hand, was furnished with a single yellow ashtray on a battered dinette set, a generic print of desert scenery on the wall, a small carpet by the front door that no one would be tempted to steal. There was a bed and a dresser, and an oversized chair that might have been cocoa colored once.

A little worse than my own place, I thought, but not much.

I placed the single personal furnishing I had brought with me on the table in place of the ashtray: a perfect nautilus shell that made me feel better each time I held it. I had purchased it in Santa Monica when a gift store was going out of business. Normally, the owner had said, these sell for sixty dollars, but he gave it to me for ten. I loved to pick it up and turn it over and over in my hands, feeling the varying textures, admiring its blushing hues, and finally placing the opening against my ear to listen to the rush and flow of air/water sighing through its chambers.

I dreamed that night of going through piles and piles of photographs, Mrs. Moreno's high-pitched voice saying, Here! No, here! Here!

I did not know what I was looking for.

The next morning I went straight to the Arizona State Museum to see if the photo archivist was in. I waited about forty-five minutes while the archivist finished another meeting.

"You're certainly welcome to look at what we have," she said. "There is a set of photographs that Thomas Hinton took in northern Mexico, but no one has been through them in years. They are not indexed, and it will take me a while to find them. Why don't you call me on Wednesday?"

I thanked her and promised I would. I asked about the photographer whose name I had, Corey McAllister.

The archivist went over to a computer terminal and looked up the name. "No, we don't have anything," she said. "But you might check the Historical Museum across the street."

"He's supposed to be famous," I said.

"Well, he may have been, but we don't have anything on him in the computers," said the archivist. "On the other hand, we have thousands of documents that haven't been entered. We just don't have the budget to do it, so we concentrate on the information that people request the most."

I crossed the street to the Historical Museum, only to find that it was closed on Tuesdays. I would have to wait until the next day.

I drove to a shopping mall — slowing at each intersection to read the unfamiliar street names — to pick up dish soap and a few more groceries. The mall looked just like all the malls in California. There was a display of metal and plastic picture frames in front of a drugstore. Each held a cheap reproduction of an old photo, a lovely woman in a high-necked lace blouse. I picked one up and looked at her, wondering if she had been a real person, and what she would think if she knew that she was now used to sell frames.

In the afternoon I went back to Mrs. Moreno's house, rang the doorbell and set off the predictable barking of Chulito. I wondered how I would translate Chulito if I were asked. Little Beloved?

Again, the door opened with barking and general pandemonium while I explained who I was. Having older relatives had prepared me for this, too. Again, Mrs. Mendoza eventually let me pass to the crimson parlor. Today promised to be a repeat of the previous day, and I tried to make myself comfortable on the couch. I couldn't decide if it was too high off the floor or too low, and kept shifting forward to the edge and back to try and press my aching back into the curvy pillows.

This time, however, Mrs. Mendoza brought out a different cardboard box and allowed me to actually pick individual photos up out of it with her, so things went a little faster. Comparing each photo to the one from Monday of the woman in the studio wearing glasses, I tried to convey what we were looking for.

I also got a better look at the first photo. It was taken in a studio, and the woman was leaning one elbow on a white column, probably plaster or painted wood. A heavy tapestry was draped artfully behind her. On the back of the photo was the imprint, FREEWATER & McALLISTER—DENVER AND TUCSON, but no date.

"This," I said, pointing to the imprint. "This is what we are looking for. Photos that have this on the back."

Again, Mrs. Mendoza held the photo before her, now turned over, and moved it back and forth before her failing eyes. I wondered how much she could really see, and how much had long since passed into the realm of shadow and memory.

"Oh, yes," she said. "I remember this." And then she looked blank.

Nevertheless, each day Mrs. Mendoza produced a few more boxes and albums of photos, saying that her invisible son had helped her get more out of storage in one of the back rooms.

I was tempted to help her sort the others into some sort of order, but from experience with my own family, I knew that this would be impossible. I had found that most people prefer the disorder of their belongings and considered me something of a neat freak. I wasn't sure why. Perhaps the notion that things could one day be organized was more empowering than facing the actual task of sorting and classifying. Or maybe it implied that their lives could be ordered as well.

This seemed to hold true for people in libraries and museums, too. Each day, I spent the morning doing research for Reuben based on a list of names of Jesuit priests, American explorers, and Mexican historians. Each archive was organized in a different manner and had a different method for allowing access to its materials. Each employee, I found, was very good at one thing and not very good at anything else. They resented questions outside of their particular field and made me sign forms before I could see most of the material. I thought about how intimidated most people would be to even come in here looking for information on the past, and how the process was set up to screen out amateurs, but I didn't say anything. These people were trained to preserve, not share. From the research documents and the archivists, I obtained the names of more historians and anthropologists, some of them even alive.

I loved the work. For the first time in over a year, I felt that I could work in peace, without fear that he would come in and try some stunt. I even began to relax around the male archivists, realizing that all they cared about was that I not mess up their materials. When they saw how respectful I was of the old papers, and how I never questioned whatever arcane rules they had made up in their particular division, they began to leave me alone more and more with the materials.

They don't know who I am, I thought. They think I am just a normal person instead of an emotional wreck who has been contemplating murder for the last several weeks.

I began to sleep at night, careful of course, to lock my doors. I was sure that he had obtained my address and wouldn't put it past him to suddenly show up and demand to see me, but the possibility seemed more abstract as the days went on. I dreamed about the research, vivid dreams of the Sonoran Desert, hearing the sounds of birds I had only read about, smelling the stink of hot muddy streets in the towns, the vegetative smell of slow rivers winding through small villages in Mexico, their banks lined with willows, girls dipping ollas for water that they carried home on their heads.

I saw that each explorer, each anthropologist, each adventurer, came with a set of ideas in his head. They were all men, of course. The priests came prepared to be shocked by ancient marriage customs. The adventurers were looking for the most lurid practices they could find, and were disappointed to come across farmers dressed like other Mexicans. One of the anthropologists spent a long time traveling from village to village in search of the Opata and was always told that they lived in the *next* village, although all the people looked alike.

Another spent a long time in one village, carefully studying their social customs and mores. According to the preface to his report, he had promised the villagers anonymity and had changed not only the name of the tribe and village in his report, but also the river valley where they lived, so that looking it up in the indexes was completely useless. I came across the monograph quite by chance, because someone had hand-written notes about it into another study. I wondered what would drive an entire people to seek refuge under an assumed name.

The anthropologist remained a complete outsider during his entire stay, and his report sounded gloomy and morose. He didn't see much of a future for these people. He didn't think much of their present. But it was clear from his omissions that they felt the same way about him. Who was going to invite this guy to a fiesta?

✝

Next Year in Magdalena

After going upstairs and down hallways, around numerous cor-
ners and asking directions and writing various names and titles
on small scraps of paper in pencil—since I was not allowed to
use a pen in the museums or archives of Arizona—I found a
semi-retired historian who had heard of the Opata. Actually,
most of the people I contacted had heard of the Opata but
didn't seem to know anything about them that was less than
five hundred years old. But this man seemed to know something about them as real people, not historical figures. He sat
casually in a corner of a vast room, surrounded by piles of
books and papers, with an air that suggested he had been waiting there for the precise moment when I would find him.

"Oh yes," he said. "They lived in the river valleys of Sonora.
They had some of the best land in Mexico. They were very
prosperous. And until the Porfiriato, it was good to be identi-
fied as Indian."

"But where did they go?" I asked. "Where can we get photos
of the Opata for this book?"

"Oh, they're still there," he said, "but the Mexican government has yet to come to terms with her indigenous people, so
Mexico really doesn't recognize them at all."

"What about Opata in the United States? Aren't there com-
munities like the Yaqui have?"

He thought for a moment. "Everyone wanted their land," he
said. "Many came north, starting with the indigenous uprisings
in the eighteen hundreds. Each time the Mexican government
sent troops in to quell an uprising, each time Mexicans moved
in to take title to their land, they usually came north. If you
worked the land, you were supposed to be able to keep title to
it, as an indigenous person. But if they made it impossible for
you to work the land, harassing you, then the government
could take it.

"The United States needed a lot of labor at that time. They
were building the railroads, starting farms in California, picking
crops all over the country. The United States did not have
enough people willing to do the hard work to keep up with the
growth and industrialization of the country. The railroads were
even bringing people in from China and Ireland. That's when
the Opata and the Yaqui left their homelands and came north to
work. They are all over the Southwest, the Midwest, parts of
the East. They are everywhere. But people thought of them as
Mexican, since they spoke Spanish. And they certainly didn't
have any reason to tell people they were Indian."

I thought about that. I had once met a woman who said she
was Yaqui and Norwegian and had grown up in Idaho. There
might be people in Chicago who had come from these villages I
had been reading about. People in Omaha and the San Joaquin
Valley and San Francisco. People in Kansas who had settled out
of the railroad business. People in Yakima who had come for
the crops and stayed. I thought about my father's family, who
had come north from central Mexico with their entire village

and settled in California. They had re-created the village right down to the layout of the streets, the church facing east. The historian was right. They could be everywhere.

I struggled to think about what that would mean in more specific terms. A man named, say, Victor Rangel from Chicago taking off his Florsheims to put on huaraches for the pilgrimage to Magdalena. Florinda Gomez putting away the heavy gloves she used to pick asparagus, loading up the kids in the back of the camper shell and driving all night to make it to the border in two days. Someone named Inez Dawson in Detroit telling her husband she was going on a business trip for five days before booking a flight to Tucson. All of these people converging on Sonora for the time between October and Christmas — to catch up with family, visit the churches and graveyards, stock up on spices unavailable in the north, and head back. Back to the scattering across North America, to a place that each called home, if only in this life.

And I thought about the ones who didn't know, the ones whose parents had thought it best not to tell them. No longer Indian, they had become Mexican. No longer Mexican, they had become Spanish. No longer Spanish, they had become — what?

I remembered a story about a lost cousin, the one whose mother had taken him away when he was little. His dad, in the military, had beat both of them until the Anglo mother took her little boy and disappeared into the vast landscape of America, into the highways and the folds of the mountains and the anonymity of another name. What had she told him about his dark eyes? His skin like almonds and peaches? Somewhere in a town like St. Louis or Tampa or Minneapolis was a man, now in his forties, who didn't realize that there was a river valley in Mexico that knew his true name. Were he to visit there, it would recognize him as hijo.

When I pulled up in front of San Xavier del Bac, my first impression was of a Middle Eastern mosque. It had three gleaming towers and looked huge from the outside. It was surrounded by high, white walls, and near the highway was a small hill with a cross at the top. People were making their way up and back along a circuitous trail, perhaps visiting the stations of the cross on the way. Nothing about the trek appealed to me in the growing heat. I put on sunglasses and made my way through the parked cars. I felt myself grow nervous as I got closer to the church, unsure if I would be welcome or just part of a tourist scene.

As I neared the main sanctuary, a spill of people emerged from an earlier service. At the door stood a large bucket full of water containing something green. An older woman with hair down her back to the ground reached in and pulled out what turned out to be a palm frond, which she tore into strips and quickly plaited into a cross. Others did the same, and as the woman held up her cross, a priest emerged and blessed her, it, and the others as they held their crosses towards him. Sensing my hesitation, a woman stepped directly in front of me and began to take pictures. The crowd milled like fish in a pond as the church continued to empty through a narrow doorway and people outside tried to enter. I grabbed a bit of wet palm as I passed the bucket and entered the dark church.

I walked in and took a seat to the right side of the sanctuary, barely able to see what I was doing. People continued to stream into the church for the next twenty minutes, holding babies and pulling small children behind them. I was next to a well-dressed woman who appeared to be in her forties. The woman sat quietly, concentrating on the front of the church. Copying those around me, I took my palm frond and tried to weave it into a small cross. It was pretty crude compared to those of the others, who seemed to know exactly what they were doing, but it held together.

The church had recently been renovated, and its interior walls gleamed with paintings, saints and snakes and symbols that could have come as easily from the Cabala as the Sonoran Desert. More people came in, bunching up at the back as they scanned the sanctuary for seats. A low-slung dog wandered unheeded down the aisle. The noise level grew and grew, and when it was time for the service to start, the Franciscan priest looked in exasperation at the congregants. I could tell he wanted the tourists to get out, and finally asked people to either be seated for the Mass or step outside.

Two huge Papago guitarists stood behind the priest, and a choir to his right began to sing under the direction of a small Anglo woman in glasses. Families continued to file in, looking as though they had driven a long way. There were men in Stetsons and new jeans, girls in Spandex dresses and big hair. Babies screamed. The hymns were all in Spanish, which the congregation knew and the priest did not.

As soon as the singing started, the nervousness I had felt upon nearing the church condensed into tears in my eyes. The hymns pulled on me in a way that I did not understand. I clutched tightly at the palm leaf cross in my hands. As the noise and the unfamiliar sensation of so many people surged around me, I felt that I needed something to hang on to. The familiar panic of imminent danger began to tint the edges of my vision, but I knew that he would not come here, would not subject himself to a place where he would not understand anything that was going on. I tried to remember to keep breathing so that I would not suddenly burst into sobs. If the woman next to me was aware of my distress, she did not show it. She sat quietly, staring straight ahead, almost straining, as though she expected to see something very important at the far, dim end of the church.

The Mass was in English, which the priest knew but most of the people did not. I stood when the others stood, sat when they sat. The responses were sluggish and indistinct, a great, unformed rumbling that started at the front of the church and died out somewhere in the back several seconds later. I realized that most people were not here for the Mass. They were waiting for something else. People who wanted to take Communion went to the front of the church. I remained in my seat, as did the woman next to me. Most of the people who went up were women, with most of the men remaining seated. Unbelievers or merely unconfessed? I wondered.

After the service, most of the people went outside, but about one hundred formed a line that began at the reclining statue of Saint Francis, which occupied a recess to the left of the altar, and snaked across the front of the church. I joined it, mostly to get a good look at the saint, as did the woman who had been seated beside me. These people were here not for the Mass but to ask favors of Saint Francis.

As I got closer, I could see a young mother pressing her newborn's face against the recumbent figure of the saint. People prayed and stroked the statue, speaking gently to it, then lifted its wooden head in their right hands two or three times before laying it back gently on its embroidered pillow. Tiny medallions and handwritten notes covered its clothing, representing favors either asked or granted by the saint.

I drew closer. I wasn't just in line to see the statue, I realized, but was not sure why I was here, what I needed that Saint Francis could offer. What was he in charge of? The priest would have said it was a statue of Saint Francis of Assisi, but the people also revered it as a combination of Saint Francis Xavier and Father Kino—the protector of the poor, the spiritual father, and the friend of nature all rolled into one. I struggled with unformed questions as I watched the others petition him, but couldn't seem to clear my head of a sort of buzzing. Perhaps it was all the prayers going up around me, clogging the long-distance lines to Heaven. At the statue, I found myself thanking the saint, thanking God, but I didn't know for what. Lifting the statue's head three times as I had seen others do, I almost staggered with its surprising weight, as though invisible roots tugged at the supine body and connected it to the earth through the stone floor of the church. I felt odd touching it, lifting its head as though it were an infant, or an invalid. I learned later that those who lacked faith were supposed to be unable to lift it.

I was still fighting tears as I walked away from the niche containing the wooden Saint Francis. Wiping my eyes, I stopped to collect myself before going out into the burning sun and looked out across the sea of people still filling the church. It was then I realized who I was seeing—the Opata. These were not the resident Papago, large and well-formed, but small-boned people from Sonora who had crossed the border for the day, or now lived in Tucson. They were here to visit their oldest friend, San Francisco. They were here, with me, in this sanctuary. And as they left the church, they exchanged the greeting "Next time in Magdalena." Unable to make the pilgrimage to visit Saint Francis in their sacred Sonoran village, they had visited this one near Tucson, this time, this year. But next year, well, God only knew what next year would bring.

I had received my unspoken, unknown wish: I had found the Opata, alive and well in the place they had always lived, since the time of their ancestors—the Sonoran Desert. Only, I thought, standing in a slight daze outside in the bright sun, they did not know who they were. Or if they did, they would not tell me, as their ancestors and relatives had refused to tell others. The ancient rituals were there, perhaps even remnants of the old language, but overlain with new pickup trucks, makeup, country-western music, and television. This was survival, I realized. This was how you stayed alive in a world that did not want you, or at least wanted your land without you on it. You kept your head low and prayed to Saint Francis.

I wanted to follow these people home, be invited for dinner, look at their family albums. I wanted to see their kids and hear about their grandparents, but already the dusty lot was emptying of cars and trucks as people went to fast-food restaurants before going shopping or heading back home to Phoenix or Tucson or Nogales. I bought fry bread sprinkled with cheese for sale in a ramada outside the church before getting in my rental car.

As I drove carefully out of the pot-holed parking area, I felt very much alone for the first time on the trip. I realized that I was one of the few people there by myself, not surrounded by family and friends. Me, I reminded myself as I drove away, back to Tucson, and the woman who had sat next to me, there by herself to ask a favor of Saint Francis. I wondered what it might have been. Could anyone be more troubled than I am? Could anyone's life be harder? Of course it could, I thought, suddenly bitter. But who could stand it?

A Photograph

By Tuesday of the next week, Mrs. Mendoza and I had un-
earthed five photographs with the imprint of Freewater &
McAllister on the back. We had gone through what seemed like
piles of boxes and albums, and I went back to my apartment
each day exhausted from speaking loudly and cheerfully to Mrs.
Mendoza, straining to look at photos in the older woman's shaking hands, from kneeling and getting up and standing in awkward positions. I finally convinced her to let me write notes on
the outsides of the boxes, just to keep them straight. Otherwise,
Mrs. Mendoza was just as likely to pull one out from two days
earlier and start in on it as though it was completely new.

Of the five with the photographer's imprint, two were taken
outside of the studio. One was of a lovely young woman with
her foot up on the running board of a carriage. It seemed a dar-
ing pose, and she had a look of mischief and adventure in her
eyes. Perhaps she was about to embark on a journey. The other
was of a corral, which was what the yard behind the houses
used to be called, and which actually served as a corral. A bull

or cow could be seen in one corner, a young boy running into the frame from the other side. In the back, somewhat in the shadows, was a carriage. The subject of the photo was unclear. The boy? The bull? The corral itself?

One of the photographs was very plain, with no backdrop visible. It was of a middle-aged woman, not quite looking at the camera.

When Mrs. Mendoza first pulled it out, she almost set it down with the large pile of photos that did not bear the photographer's imprint.

"Wait!" I said. "What's that on the back?"

Sure enough, there was the gold lettering.

"Yes, but it is only a woman who worked for us," said Mrs. Mendoza.

Again, she tried to set it down, but this time I intercepted it.

"What was her name?"

"Concha," said Mrs. Mendoza. "She took care of my older brothers and sisters, but I don't remember her."

"But you do," I said.

Mrs. Mendoza took the photo back from me. "It was all before I was born. I heard some stories about her. She was an Indian from Sonora."

Mrs. Mendoza hesitated, concentrating on the serious face, the broad shoulders, moving the photo towards and away from her.

"I think she became embarazada."

"You mean pregnant?"

"Yes. She wasn't married. But the father was Irish," she said, brightening, "so her baby probably wasn't as dark."

I looked closely at the photo.

"She doesn't look very dark, at least in this picture."

"Well, some of them were and some of them weren't. But the *real* Indians were very dark, casi negros."

I took notes. "What kind of an Indian was she?"

"Oh, those that used to work for my father. They were from Sonora, and hard-working. Not like those from here. They were Opata."

I waited until she set the photo down before taking it gently. The woman looked both scared and obstinate, dignified yet aggrieved, as though thinking, *Fine. I'll live this life, I'll wear these clothes, I'll stand still for this picture if you want me to. But you can't make me like it, and you can't make me like you.*

I stared at the photo. Something about the line of the woman's face seemed familiar. It brought back half-formed memories of going through old boxes at an aunt's house on a rainy day.

I glanced over at Mrs. Mendoza, who had lapsed into a rare silence.

"Will you let me take this one with me today? I want to compare it with some at the museum."

Mrs. Mendoza roused herself. "Yes, I guess so. Are you done with these others?" she said, pointing to the small stack of Freewater & McAllister photos.

"Oh, no," I said. Reuben had asked me to try and get them from Mrs. Mendoza, even offer her money. He was thinking of a book featuring photographers of the Old West.

"I think the editor is interested in all of them. Did you tell Deedee that you would give them to the museum?"

"I don't know." Mrs. Mendoza looked a little surprised. "I'll have to ask my son."

"I think they were willing to pay a little. If not, they will want to make copies of them."

"Copies?"

"Yes, they can copy them at the university without hurting the original photos."

"But you would have to take them?"

"Yes. For a little while. Then I would bring them back."

"Well, then, I will have to ask my son."

"Okay. And this one? Can I take it with me today? Or not?" I could not help myself. Of course, this is what I had been looking for. The museum was full of photos of people from the Sonoran desert taken by Thomas Hinton, but because no one had matched his notes to the photos, none of them were definitively Opata. This one might not be either, but if I could keep working on Mrs. Mendoza, maybe she could come up with something else about the woman. At least Mrs. Mendoza was alive and willing to talk.

"You like that one?" she asked.

"Yes," I said. "I don't know why."

"Well then, you keep it," she said. "That woman was once very dear to my family."

And she pressed the photo into the palm of my hand, patting my fingers closed around it. This is what Reuben had hoped for, I'm sure, that I would be able to gain Mrs. Mendoza's confidence in a way that someone else might not. Still, I was touched by her obvious feeling.

That evening, I dragged a chair out onto the narrow balcony of the apartment. With a glass of iced tea beside me, I looked and looked at the photograph. I couldn't understand why I was so drawn to this obstinate-looking woman. She was big, with square shoulders. I had come to think of the Opata women as small, with birdlike bones. Maybe Mrs. Mendoza was mistaken; maybe this woman was Papago.

But she had no reason to identify her as Opata if she wasn't, unless there was a status difference among the types of Indians among the Mexicans. Outside of the Apaches, I hadn't found any. In truth, all the the Sonoran people were pretty closely related. The Apaches stole children, and the villagers kept and raised the Apache children as their own after they caught and killed adult Apaches. One story was that Geronimo had himself been kidnapped from a Sonoran village and raised as an Apache, so maybe he was Opata. It was a falsehood to think that all the people of a tribe were going to look typically one way or another. Concha could just be a big Opata, like Tánori, the head of the tribe in the 1850s.

Mrs. Mendoza had said the Opata were hard-working, so maybe they had a reputation among the Mexican ranchers who had been born in Sonora, or maybe they had ties of family — a family of Opata who had worked for more than one generation of a Mexican family.

"Concha." I said, feeling the name in my mouth. It seemed such a fragile name for this woman, this mountain of stubbornness contained in a single photo. I knew I shouldn't have the photo outside, even in the weak light before sunset, so I rose to go inside.

I remembered seeing a photo when I was little. A woman in a long white dress stood on the left. It appeared to be a portrait of a woman for her wedding, but as I looked at the ragged photo, I realized that the groom had been torn away. Whoever had severed the man from his bride had not even bothered to use scissors, but had just ripped the photo in two and ruined it as any sort of keepsake.

I had wondered why the photo hadn't been thrown away if it was so offensive. I asked my mother about it, and she said the woman in the photo was her own grandmother. Then she said that the woman's husband had left her. I went away and thought about that, then came back and asked if the man was not, then, her grandfather. My mother had refused to answer, saying it was a long story and she didn't want to talk about it. She acted upset. I realized then that my mother herself had mutilated the photograph, the same way her own marriage had been torn in two.

I also remembered the way my parents had treated each other when we all lived together. The fights when my sister, Cassie, and I had wedged ourselves behind the bed in our room and tried to cover our ears from the ugly insults that hurt us as much as our parents tried to hurt each other. I didn't ask any more that day. I must have sensed dangerous ground using the radar that children develop in self-defense. There were a lot of things I didn't understand then, and half a photo was just one more to add to the pile. My parents had divorced when I went away to college and my sister was already married.

I really didn't know very much about my family. People from Mexico, my grandmother born in Arizona—was it Tucson or Nogales? Maybe it was Phoenix. Or maybe it was that town in New Mexico way down in a corner of the map. They were people who had moved and moved again as war, starvation, work, and fate led them from town to town, city to city. Here were a few relatives, there a few others. My father's family was the same way, working all over the United States for the railroad before settling in California. At this remove, we were all separated by name, by religion, by who my aunts and uncles had married. I knew that some of them had Anglicized their names and tried to blend in.

Cassie had lightened her hair since she was in high school, and I remember my mother used to get mad at me when she thought I was getting too dark in the sun. My sister got married right out of high school, a man with blond hair and blue eyes. Once in a while, he had a job, but the marriage allowed Cassie to ditch the last name of Ríos and use a bland, all-American name that required no explanation, did not bring on an inquisition from the teacher or the employer or the nurse or doctor or store clerk. I had always answered these questions, with some notion that enlightenment is a good thing, but had discovered that others, in turn, don't like to answer such questions, and almost always balk if the tables are turned.

Until now, I had felt that my family existed on the frayed hem of history—jetsam left by the high tide on the beach of time. In spite of all the brave talk about multiculturalism and diversity, no one really cared what happened to Mexican Americans in the Southwest as long as they stayed in their place. But I wasn't sure what that place was anymore. Fontana had offered no opportunities, Irvine had been okay, but Los Angeles was openly hostile to anyone without money or connections. Here in Tucson, at least, everyone looked like me and didn't have to be told how to spell my last name.

When I got to the museum the next day, there were three messages waiting, all from World Educational Resources. I called Robert.

"Boy, is he pissed," he said.

"Why?"

"He can't find anything. He says you took numbers out of his Rolodex."

I sighed. "Why would I do that? I'm not even sure I know where his Rolodex is. That office is like a cave."

"Well, he can't find anything, and he's blaming you."

"Look on my desk," I said. "Maybe the numbers he wants are in *my* Rolodex."

"Well, you better hurry back. It has not been very happy around here."

"I thought it would be much happier without me."

"He's afraid of losing your position. Marci did not work out. She quit last week."

"She *quit?* How can a temp quit? Aren't they under contract or something?"

"She threw herself on Mrs. Osaka's mercy and begged to be transferred. She couldn't take it."

"Wimp," I said, but my heart sank. All the old things came rushing back. I hadn't realized how much better I had felt, how normal, for the last few days. I had been eating and sleeping. My skin was turning a normal color from going outside during the day.

"You'll just have to do what you can until the end of the week," I told Robert. "I'll be back on Monday."

"He wants to know when your flight is coming in."

"I don't know," I said. "I don't have my ticket with me. What am I supposed to do, find his Rolodex for him at the airport?"

But I knew what he wanted. He wanted to be there before anyone else, to get to me first and start weaving his web of fake concern and coercion around me. To give me a ride and try to carry my bags into my apartment and make himself at home. He was afraid I might get away from him, now that Marci had not "worked out."

The rest of the morning at the museum I had a bad taste in my mouth. I looked through many more photos from Sonora — girls in regular dresses like those in the United States, but standing in front of dome-shaped, grass or palm-covered structures. Serious-looking men standing on boards set about four feet above the ground, part of some ceremony. Men dancing in a dusty, dry open space before a church that appeared half caved in. All of the photos were numbered but didn't match up with the field notes in the other building. If I could have looked at the notes and the photos at the same time, this might have been easier.

I wrote down several questions for the photo archivist, but she didn't come in while I was there. No one seemed to know where she was or when she was expected.

I only had iced tea for lunch. It was hotter now, and the students at the university were all wearing shorts. All day I kept seeing someone out of the corner of my eye—just slipping around a corner or out of sight. The glimpse was fleeting—a white shirt, the pale sole of a shoe. But instead of filling me with panic, as these glimpses had for a long time, they made me want to meet this person, to have our paths finally cross.

I dreamed that night about the man in the coffee shop, the one who might actually be nice. He had bought a rusty old Corvette. I hadn't seen him in a while and we had a lot of catching up to do. He looked a little different; his hair was messed up. He looked, perhaps, more real.

We went for a drive in his new car, out to some park in the mountains. He had decided to return to college and get a two-year degree to learn how to make bifocals. Whatever he had been doing hadn't work out. Then he reached out to me and pulled me to him and we made love, or were about to.

That's how dreams are. Nothing ever quite happens, but you assume it's going to. It's as though your mind stops wasting energy on the image once it thinks you understand what's going on. It was a mild night, warm, and the top was down on the Corvette, and I could tell that he had wanted to do this for a long time but had been afraid to. Afraid of what? Afraid to try and touch me. Afraid of me, of course. That I would say no. But I didn't. So maybe it did happen after all. In my dreams.

I woke up wondering if I would ever want a person, a real person, to touch me again.

Waiting Room

The idea refused to wholly reveal itself, but continued to float just below the surface of my thoughts, like a ship just beyond the horizon of consciousness, or a rotten water lily sinking beneath the surface of a pond.

So this was the end of it, if not a real ending: a bench in a waiting room, the glow of vending machines, the disinterested glances of strangers to see if you were dangerous, or worse, insane, before taking a seat in your proximity. Most people, I noticed, chose to move on.

There was a dull throbbing in my veins, my bones. I dreaded the thought of spending my days back in that office. If I didn't go back, then what? I could get a job as a waitress at a truck stop in Arizona, a place where I could wear comfortable white shoes and call people Honey. With enough hairspray and makeup, I thought, I could insulate myself from any come-on, any insult. I wondered if those words, insult and insulate, had a common root: *insultado*. Could you say it in Spanish? Any word could be made to sound right in Spanish.

No one, I realized, would care if I didn't return to L.A. I had finished the research for the book, finding more and better pictures than anyone could have dreamed. The photos and the stories behind them were so good, in fact, that they probably merited a book in their own right. My boss would find some way to jump on it and claim all the credit. He would make sure everyone thought it was his idea. I wondered whether or not Reuben or Ellen would protest. Probably not. They were there for the duration, and intended to earn their retirements without any complications from him.

No, no one would miss me, and there were a dozen — no, fifty desperate people who would take my job in a second. People who would do anything to get in on the ground floor of the publishing business, even work in that office. He would be charming at first, like he was with me. Polite, even, in a Southern gentleman sort of way before the next step and the next. No one would stop him, but maybe the next editorial assistant would handle it better, put him off smoothly, or better yet, just Mace him in an elevator one night when he rubbed up against her. Maybe then, just maybe, the others would come forward and say, *Yes, he did it to me, too,* just as they had in private when I finally started crying in the women's rest room, the last place on earth, that day, that seemed safe to me.

I pulled a manila envelope from my pack and took out my favorite photo. I had an extra copy made for myself when Mrs. Moreno agreed to let the Arizona State Museum make copies. In it, a tall woman stands on a busy street. She is dressed in black and carries several bundles. Her hair is back in a bun, showing her long Indian face and slanted eyes. The woman has that slightly stooped posture that I've come to associate with people who think they are too tall, or with women who think they are too visible, a shrinking into themselves. Nevertheless, the woman has a sort of pride, of dignity, that shines through this, that hints at an indominable nature in the face of every possible adversity. Maybe a nature that was too willful, that brought her more pain than someone else might have brought on herself.

The woman in the photo is looking towards the camera but not really at it. I wasn't sure if that was the custom of the time, or just a trick of the photographic methods in use at the turn of the century.

The woman is neither happy nor sad. Rather, her face is too guarded to tell. She had made herself an exterior mask that hides her true self, and I tried to imagine the life that she might have led.

All I knew, from the information Mrs. Moreno had given me, was that the woman's name was Concha, and that the photograph was taken in 1893.

Concha moved slowly down the street, favoring her left ankle. I wondered where she was going—maybe home. Someone waited for her there, not a husband, but maybe a child.

The street was full of the noise of late afternoon, early evening. I noticed how the town had come alive after the searing heat of the afternoon. Somewhere a guitar was carelessly strummed. People were laughing and joking. Concha walked on through the dusty streets, lifting each foot carefully over the uneven bricks and stones. She passed by people without them looking at her, or she at them.

I imagined that she was hungry after working all day. Where did she work? In a house like Mrs. Mendoza's?

Concha held up her head and walked.

And then she heard a voice behind her. It was under the rumbling of wagons, the creaking of carriages, under the shrill voice of a woman who thought she had been cheated, the coming and going of many people, shouting, laughing, dogs barking—but she heard it, nevertheless.

Someone was calling Concha. She stopped walking and slowly turned. I could not understand the words, but Concha began to search the faces in the crowd as the voice cried out harshly, persistently, like the cawing of a crow. Concha finally saw someone and began to walk back towards him. She seemed to fight the tide of people now, more going the way she had gone than the way she was now moving, being jostled at every step.

Concha saw that the man was seated on a board on wheels, and as she approached, she saw that his stained pant legs were cut off short, that his legs ended above his knees, and the stumps were bound to the board with wide leather straps. I did not recognize this man, had seen no one like him in Mrs. Moreno's photographs or the archives.

The man placed both hands on the ground, the knuckles cushioned by rags, and propelled himself towards Concha with a peculiar hopping motion — all torso, all muscle; a beggar, I thought.

To my surprise, Concha fell to her knees next to this man and embraced him.

"Dios mío," she said, over and over. "Dios mío."

He began to talk with her, and eventually they began to move through the crowd — Concha walking as the man propelled himself forward on his board.

I thought of trains, and thought perhaps something had happened to the man on a train that would have cut both legs off. Or maybe he was born that way. I could not tell. Was this Concha's husband? Had he been gone a long time? Another relative from Sonora?

Concha wept as they walked, and I realized that she did have feelings that she could show, that the careful mask could be pushed aside to show the real person inside. But not for a photographer, not for a stranger.

I felt as though I was walking behind them, following them through the crowd and sometimes losing sight of them, only to see them just ahead.

They made their way through the busiest part of town, then to a lane that was just adobe dirt full of rocks. I did not recognize any of it, but I wasn't sure that I would recognize the Tucson of that era anyway. Everything had changed.

They came to a steep set of steps that led up the side of a small hill, and I wondered if the man could go up them. At the top was a doorway with a blanket hung over it.

Concha smiled at him and went up by herself, calling out as she went. After a while she came out again carrying things wrapped in cloth. A girl was with her, maybe her daughter.

The three of them went farther down the rutted lane and settled themselves on a cloth that they spread on the ground. The man remained a little apart, a stranger to the girl, and took out his tobacco to smoke.

Concha built a fire in the sand and put dishes of food on it. I wondered if they always ate like this or if it was something special to accommodate the man on the board.

They talked and talked, but as the light faded, it was harder to hear what they were saying, as though the lack of light dampened the sound. I understood that they were talking about the past, about people they had known. I recognized the words "Tepupa" and "Casas Grandes." I was sure now that they were from Sonora, but not of too much more. It had been a long time since they had seen each other.

Finally the girl, who couldn't have been more than twelve or thirteen, put her head down in her mother's lap. She was lighter than her mother, less Indian. Maybe this was the child that Concha bore when she went away from the Mendozas' house. I tried to think if I had seen any pictures of this girl, but I had looked at so many photos over the past two weeks that my head was in a swirl. The adults continued to talk as the air cooled and darkened and the fire became brighter in the deepening dusk.

I struggled to stay with the scene, to find out all that I could about these people before it got too dark, but the words were in a dialect that was strange to me. They took on a life of their own and flew about me like birds. Cicadas came awake in the deepening night and formed a competition with the words — cranking up over and over again in their repetitive song. I longed to go and sit close by the fire so that I could hear better, but I couldn't seem to move.

I tried to lift my feet, then just my hand, before I jerked my head up. It was too quiet. I had been dozing. I looked to see if my suitcase was still on the floor beside me, and it was. I laid a hand on it just to reassure myself, to feel something solid.

The concourse was empty and dark. I looked at my watch and saw that my plane had left almost an hour ago. I jumped up, grabbing my suitcase, and ran to the airline desk. It was empty and closed. They had just left me there, sleeping.

I really had missed my flight. After the initial panic, my heartbeat slowed and my eyes adjusted to the dim light. A candy wrapper lay on the floor near the chairs, the mangled remains of today's newspaper. What was today? A Wednesday, the most anonymous day of the week.

I suddenly felt anonymous, and liked it. No one knew where I was. I was sure I could get another flight. Or maybe not. I could return to L.A. or not. What would I leave if I didn't go back? A rented studio, some clothes, a television, a cheap car. I could go back and get the car and drive back.

I wasn't sure why I felt this way. It was just another assignment. Yet I felt as if I had been given a chance to change the direction of my life.

The photo. I looked around and found the photo of Concha face down on the dirty tile floor. It had fallen from my hand while I was asleep. Picking it up and dusting it off, I felt that, at the moment, this picture was the most valuable possession I owned. I clasped it to my chest, wiping the dust off on my T-shirt, then reinserted it into the manila envelope with the other photos and placed the envelope in my pack.

I put on the backpack, picked up my suitcase, and began walking towards the main terminal, still uncertain what to do. The lights in the candy machine glowed brightly for a moment as I neared it, as though possessed by a really good idea, then blinked out.

Los Angeles

People were so nice to me when I returned.

"You're famous," said Robert. "Everyone's been talking about how you got those photos from that old lady. Charmed her socks off. She didn't have a chance."

"It wasn't quite like that."

I had been back from Tucson for a week, but I still found myself distracted and absent-minded. I realized that I missed the intense light of the Sonoran Desert—light unaccompanied by a proximity to water. The light in Sonora reduced every item on which it fell to its elemental self—light and dark, substance and shadow, reflection and absorption. I thought I understood the photographer's attraction to that place, so long ago, the need to produce something out of nothing, to try and capture the moment of existence on a piece of glass. I found myself putting up brightly colored cards or illustrations torn from magazines. Maybe I was allergic to artificial light.

An old photo left even for a minute directly in the intense light of the Arizona sun would have been lost forever. I thought about lizards shriveling on a rock. I thought about bones bleaching in an arroyo, washed down from the hill country by the last flash flood. The light reduced everything on the desert back to its elements. The desert's job, it seemed, was to re-absorb all of the life that happened onto it, to recycle matter from flesh and metal to water and stone. Nothing was wasted in that environment—everything was used.

I thought about these things as my tan faded under the fluorescent lights of World Educational Resources.

I had called my mother when I got back, intending to ask her some more questions about my grandmother. Where, ex-actly, had she been born? Who was my grandmother's father, if not the man in, or rather missing from, the photo? I left a message on the answering machine.

"Oh, I don't know, honey," my mother said when she finally returned the call. I knew the call would be short, since it was long distance. "No one ever told me very much. It didn't seem important at the time. Why do you want to know now?"

I tried to explain about the research I had been doing, about my trip to Arizona. I asked my mother if she had heard of the Opata.

"That doesn't sound familiar. I think my grandmother was Opi. Or Hopi."

I wondered if Opi was how you said Hopi in Spanish. Or a variation on Opata, who were known by several different names. There was always the language difference to confuse everything.

"I'll ask my sister," my mother said. "She knew more about it than I did. But Paul was the one who knew the most. He was always interested in that stuff."

Paul, of course, had died several years ago.

"I'll call you if I find something out," she said, and we hung up.

I had meant to ask about the torn photo but had forgotten. Or maybe I was just afraid.

One day he came out of his office abruptly.

"Do you have time to go over Karen's manuscript? Or are you too busy with this other stuff?"

Robert gave me a look like *nothing had changed* as I took paper and a pen into his office, where he slammed the door before settling behind his desk.

"You've managed to stay completely busy ever since you got back," he began. "Not one minute for me."

I kept my eyes down and said nothing.

His voice softened. "I missed you. I thought we had something special. You never even called."

Still I said nothing. I thought of the silent sweeps of the desert, how you could go all day without hearing another human voice.

"Can you have dinner with me? Or are you too fucking wonderful for me now?"

"I have a little follow-up work to do," I stammered. I really did, but I knew it sounded like a lie. "I told Ellen I would stop by her office at four-thirty, if it's okay with you, and I don't know how long it will take."

"You meeting with Ellen and Reuben?"

"At least with Ellen. I don't know about Reuben."

"Yeah. I saw how he looked at you today."

We sat in silence in the dark office. He never turned on more than a small desk lamp.

Finally I asked, "Did you have some proofreading?"

"Yeah, I had some proofreading," he said angrily, putting out his cigarette. "I've got a memo to proof to Reuben to keep his fucking hands off you."

I stood up and walked out of the office. I was trying with all of my strength not to cry but was failing.

"Uh-oh," said Robert.

The intercom on Robert's phone buzzed, and he was called in himself. I could hear them laughing every once in a while as I tried to type up my notes from Tucson. I could barely see the paper.

When I came out of the meeting with Ellen and Reuben, I felt better. I returned cautiously to the office to pick up my things and was relieved to find that everyone else had gone home. I rode downstairs in the elevator with one of the younger accountants who'd been working late, and even smiled at him and said hello. I have a right to at least be civil, I thought.

I looked forward to getting home that night. I had bought groceries and planned to fix myself a real dinner — rice and chicken with tortillas, enough to have leftovers for a couple of days instead of my usual dinners of frozen pizza and apple slices. I carefully balanced everything in the elevator.

"Here, let me get that for you," he said, taking my keys from my hand as I approached the door to my apartment.

I hadn't seen him waiting. "What are you doing here?"

"I thought we better get to work on this editing. I know how hard you worked to get stuff back from Karen, but she just returned it today." He opened my door and walked in.

"Nice place," he said, looking around. He put some papers down on my table. "Well? Are you going to just stand out there?"

I'm being ridiculous, I thought. He just wants to brag to the men at work that he was at my apartment. There. Now he can do it.

I went in and set my groceries on the counter, leaving the door open. I went in the bathroom. Normally I would have changed out of my work clothes, but I didn't want to encourage him to stay.

"Can't this wait until tomorrow?" I asked when I came out.

"You were the one who was so anxious to keep moving. And then you went off to Arizona for three weeks."

"That's because there wasn't anything to do until we got the manuscript back."

"Well, here it is. Sit down and let's get started. You owe me this time."

The front door was now shut.

After one chapter of him reading passages out loud while I marked up the manuscript, he stood up and said, "Say, Shelly, don't you have anything to drink? Anything to offer a guest?"

"There's ice water and orange juice. Would you like some?"

"Don't you have anything stronger?"

"No," I said.

"Seriously?"

I shrugged. I didn't drink and didn't see why I needed to explain that.

"Why don't I get something and come back?"

"Why don't you go home and I'll see you tomorrow at work?" I said.

"Oh, you are so funny," he said. "First you get me over to your place, then throw ice water on me."

I said nothing.

"You know," he said, getting up and moving towards me, "I could help you a lot more than Reuben can." He moved the papers I had spread out on the couch and sat next to me.

"Why are you so fixated on Reuben?" I asked. "I just did the research for one chapter of one book that they needed. He hasn't offered anything else."

"I could make sure you were an associate editor by the end of the year."

"That's nice," I said, and tried to get up.

He held my arm. "But you need to develop a better attitude."

I tried to shake him off casually, then pull away, but he held my arm tightly. He treated it like a game, laughing as I got more upset. I tried screaming, something I was never good at, and he was immensely entertained.

"You see?" he said. "It's no good. Everyone just thinks you're having fun with your boyfriend. And you are."

I swung and hit him in the face hard enough to hurt my hand, but he didn't even bleed. He slapped me just as hard without letting go. My nautilus shell rolled off the table and hit the carpeting with a dull thud.

"I don't know what you're carrying on about," he said, then smiled. "I just want to make you feel good."

Somewhere in there was the belief that if I could cast no shadow, he would be unable to harm me.

Somewhere in there was the belief that if I could keep from casting a shadow on the wall at the head of the bed, he would be unable to harm, hurt, or damage me permanently.

"Relax," he said, and pushed my shoulder down hard against the bed. "I just want to give you a little ol' back rub."

I said nothing. I was furious with myself for not staying outside. I wanted to hit him again, but there was a menace in his blunt fingers now. I had watched him use his size and position to intimidate other people at the office, both men and women. He took up a lot of room when he was angry, he would stand in your face and yell, he would make a big scene at someone else's expense. Incredibly, this approach had worked for eleven years. People gave in rather than deal with him.

"Just let me get a little more comfortable. . . ."

He stood and quickly got undressed.

I imagined myself becoming smaller and smaller, taking up less and less space until I was invisible. I tried to will myself to be somewhere else, to dissolve from this existence, this body, and appear somewhere else, anywhere—or disappear altogether.

This is the last time I will ever allow myself to be alone with this man, I promised myself. Unless I'm carrying a gun.

†

Hermana Araña

I boarded the plane, weary from lack of sleep and cold from the over air-conditioned airport. It had been a long, smoggy summer, and without a recommendation from a boss, I had been unable to find another job. No one else at World Educational Resources would even return my calls.

As I buckled my seat belt and raised my seat back, the pilot announced that his name was Herman Aranda. He encouraged the passengers to look for the exits and make themselves at home.

After liftoff, as we broke through the cloud cover and leveled off across the Mojave Desert, Hermana Araña, the pilot, the voice now more like a flute than a bass, suggested we take off our jackets and shoes. We gladly complied. Women began to congregate at the front of the plane, men at the back.

A wooden bowl was inverted in a pan of water and hit with two sticks. It made a hollow, booming sound that echoed the length of the plane, a deep, repetitive rhythm, insistent as a blackbird setting its territory. Two girls got up and began to dance, moving their feet back and forth, back and forth chicken-scratch style, but they soon subsided into shy giggles and sat down. There was no board for the men to dance on. The drum continued alone.

The men at the back of the plane began to smoke. A small bottle was produced, and three or four small earthenware cups. An old man in an old hat began to tell stories about the old days. He had a few teeth.

A woman began to pass up and down the aisle, selling silver religious trinkets, small wooden crosses, and necklaces made of desert seeds. Very powerful medicine. Blessed by Saint Francis on his feast day.

Soon it was time to fasten our seat belts. A little more money changed hands, the mescal was finished. All were quickly seated as the descent began.

The plane coasted to a stop on a long dirt field. An old woman stood laughing and waving a broom made of bundled sticks at the end of the track where the creosote bushes loomed up. The air was very clear. No buildings were to be seen.

The passengers quickly donned straw hats and sandals and picked up their bundles. Without speaking or lingering, each headed out in a different direction across the apparently trackless land. To the south, an ancient pickup waited, its engine running roughly as the driver tinkered with the distributor. A few people approached and placed their bags in the back, hoisting themselves inside.

"Where are you going?" I asked the driver in English.

He looked up at me, startled to see a new face. "Magdalena."

"¿A cómo le da?" I asked.

He relaxed slightly. "Quince dólares."

I lifted my bag over the tailgate, where those inside took it and helped me in. The tailgate appeared to be permanently welded shut. A very ugly dog let me pass before assuming its position in the back left corner.

The driver slammed the hood of the truck and collected money from each of us. Some people appeared to make this trip often, their bags full of canned goods and packaged clothing from department stores.

The drive took a long time and eventually I slept. We stopped once while the driver got more gas and examined the engine, and a few people took their things and left. I noticed that my watch was gone, and wondered when I had lost it.

It was long after dark when we arrived, but one cantina was open, light and noise spilling out into the street. I took my bag and walked towards it. The sandals chafed because they were too big. I would have to find a way to shorten the straps or go barefoot.

A woman gathered plates from a table near the window and turned away. Something in the squareness of her shoulders, the way her hands moved without hesitation, made me stop. The table remained empty.

After a time, I went inside. I set my bag on the floor and sat at the empty table covered in oilcloth. Two people talked quietly at another table, a jukebox played sad songs, and a man sat at the counter by himself, smoking and drinking coffee. Outside, dogs barked constantly. The air must have been full of ghosts. Even though I had slept in the truck, I just thought I would rest my head on my arms until the waitress came.

A loud click woke me, and I sat up to see a plate of beans and meat and rice in front of me.

"¿Algo más?" asked the woman.

"Café, por favor."

She returned with a steaming cup of coffee, milk, and raw sugar. Her hair was gathered in a bun. She wore a flowered apron, faded from much washing, over a white shirt with the sleeves rolled up, a dark skirt.

I couldn't help myself.

"I'm looking for someone," I said in my halting Spanish, cradling the hot coffee cup in my hands. "Her name was Concha Canelos, but she might have been known by something else. She came from south of here, near Tepupa."

The woman looked at me without expression, then turned away. I sighed and ate my food. It was very good.

A few minutes later the woman returned with another cup of coffee and sat down across from me. She slowly pushed off her shoes, slippers really, and I could see that her feet and ankles were thick from a lifetime of hard work. Her capable hands, almost square, were never still. I looked at the worn fingers wrapped around the coffee cup, the pinpoints of white that speckled the backs of her hands and continued up her arms. I realized that they were burn scars from years of cooking oil and lard splattering and marking her arms as she worked over a hot stove—turning tortillas, stirring beans, frying meat. They were the arms of a woman shaped by kitchen work, by the slavery of the soul to the stomach.

I also realized that I was staring, but the woman did not seem to mind. She was savoring the fact of being seated, of freeing her feet from shoes, of waiting rather than waiting upon.

As I looked for the first time full into her face, I realized that the woman was probably only about ten years older than I was. Until then I had thought she was much older. I sat up straight to meet her gaze.

"¿Quieres más?" she asked, pointing at my plate with her chin.

"No. Gracias," I answered. "But it's very good."

Now it was her turn to stare. She looked at me closely, as though searching for clues to who I was.

"Tell me," the woman said finally. "Tell me your story."